REJECTS PARADISE

Sheridan Anne
Black Widow: A Rejects Paradise Novella

Copyright © 2021 Sheridan Anne
All rights reserved
First Published in 2021
Anne, Sheridan
Black Widow: A Rejects Paradise Novella

Cover: Covers By Aura
Editing: Fox Proof Editing
Proofreading: Danielle Stansbury & Noemi Vallone
Formatting: Sheridan Anne

BLACK *widow*

CHAPTER 1
RONI

"**B**REAKING NEWS; at 4:38 pm this afternoon, Dominic Garcia, head of the Breakers Flats Black Widows escaped Longview Maximum Penitentiary for Men. He was last seen heading west towards Bellevue Springs."

A mug shot appears on the television and I stare at it with wide eyes, my heart racing a million beats an hour as I strain to hear the reporter over the loud pulsing in my ears. "Dominic is responsible for the gang war that hit the streets between Breakers Flats and Blaxlands Grove nearly seven years ago, resulting in multiple deaths, one being the leader of the West Side Wolves, Mikhail Russo. Along with charges of theft, possession of a deadly weapon, and assault. It is safe to assume that Dominic is armed and dangerous."

My hand covers my mouth as I try not to scream. This can't be happening. I was supposed to be safe. I still had three and a half years before he was out. Three and a half years before I had to run. This wasn't part of my plan.

What am I supposed to do?

He's coming for me. There's no doubt about it. I know it right down in my soul.

The reporter continues, her face draining of color, almost as though the thought of Nic being out of prison is the scariest thing she's ever encountered. She'd be right. She should be terrified. The whole fucking city should be. "Tonight, police are searching far and wide to get this dangerous criminal back behind bars where he belongs. This is a public service announcement. If you see him, do not approach, do not communicate, and do not allow him into your homes. I repeat, do not engage with this man. Flee to safety and call your local police department as soon as possible."

The screen flashes to footage of a white transport van leaving the prison, merging onto the highway, and speeding through traffic to get away. His mug shot appears again, and I suck in a breath. It's as though I'm staring straight into his eyes. I find myself hitting pause, unable to look away from his face. It's the face of my nightmares, the face that has held me captive for nearly twelve years.

I was a different person at sixteen, naive and stubborn. If I knew the hell that Dominic Garcia would rain down over me, I'd have stayed far, far away. But I was a girl and he was more than just a boy … so much more.

The minutes tick by with me sitting on my couch, staring at the screen, and taking in his face. It's just as I've always remembered. He hasn't aged a day in the seven long years since I saw him last. Though, there's a very real possibility that this is an old mug shot. I'm sure he's taken his fair share of mug shots over the years.

I go over everything that the reporter just said.

He was last seen heading west towards Bellevue Springs.

My heart races faster.

Bellevue Springs has been my home for the past nine years. I've worked here, thrived here, started a new life here. I live just outside of Bellevue Springs as only the rich and famous can afford to live there, but it doesn't mean this isn't my home.

And now he's coming.

I shoot to my feet, panic surging through me.

He could be heading this way to see his friend Ocean and meet her baby, Storm. I've kept up with her all these years, and she's become a great friend. The way she survived all the bullshit she went through was admirable, but a part of me has always wondered if I kept her close because of her connection to Dominic. Though she never knew about Nic and me, no one did. He was my best-kept secret, which is what makes this so dangerous. I'm screwed if Nic comes for me; no one would know where to look.

Nic promised that he would always come for me, and now that he's got nothing else holding his attention, I'm all he has left.

If I knew this was how it was going to end … fuck. I never would have gone there. But Nic is Nic. He's always been so charismatic, so charming, and devilishly handsome. He comes armed with a grin that could tear any woman's panties right off her body, and he's only gotten better with time. He has more tattoos than I remember, but fuck, they're my weakness.

Dominic thrives on the chase; it's his addiction. He loves having a target to focus all of his attention on. Without it, he'd be running rampant, and no one could stop him—not even his crew. He's a fucking psychotic killer looking for his next hit, and my name just appeared at the top of his list.

Don't ask me how I know; it's just a feeling, and so far, my gut has never let me down. My brother taught me two things in life; to punch first, think later, and to always trust your gut. I know I haven't seen him in at least five years, but I'm not in the business of forgetting important life-saving lessons.

I have to run, and I have to run fucking fast.

I dart to my bedroom, grabbing my suitcase on the way. I have to disappear, at least until he's caught and put back behind bars where he should be, but something tells me that will never happen. Dominic only ever does what Dominic wants to do. He got caught on purpose and played the system just like he played with my heart. The fact that he's out means that whatever threat was heading his way has finally been handled.

Dominic Garcia lives by his own law. In fact, to him, he is the law. There's no one above him, and that's part of the reason he's so terrifying. He's the perfect manipulator and knows exactly what to do and say to make anyone fall at his feet. He's the very reason I got into psychology.

I start grabbing my clothes and throwing them into my suitcase, not even taking note of what I'm packing. All that matters is getting out. I can deal with the rest later. I've rebuilt my life from nothing once before—I can do it again.

I knew my world was going to come crumbling down around me when he found me in Bellevue Springs. It was only a matter of time. I had hope that his issues with Ocean would keep him distracted, but my luck has finally run out.

The clock has stopped ticking.

It's go time.

My phone tumbles into my suitcase as I yank the charger from the outlet, grabbing whatever I can along the way. I have no idea what time he staged his little breakout. I could have hours before he makes it here, or I could only have mere seconds.

The fear of the unknown sits heavy on my heart as my mind whirls with ideas of where I should go or how I'm going to get myself out of this. He'll never stop hunting me. He'll never let me go. No matter where I end up, he'll always find me. At least, that's what he did when I left in the first place.

If only I were brave enough to tell my brother about it. He would have kept me safe, but he would have done it at the expense of his own life. I can't bring him into this. With Christian being the leader of the West Side Wolves, Dominic won't hesitate to end him. He'll take pride in it and rub it in the faces of everyone it hurts. It'll start another war, and Dominic will only rise higher. With the Wolves out of the picture, Dominic would be unstoppable. He'd dominate the whole fucking state.

After jamming my feet into old shoes and zipping up the suitcase, getting material caught in the zipper, I hurry out into my kitchen, hauling my suitcase behind me. I yank open the drawers, scrambling around and searching for the knife I'd hidden in here nearly eight years ago when his face first appeared in Bellevue Springs.

I should have prepared for this. I should have had my bag ready to go.

I thought I had time.

After pulling apart my kitchen and finally finding my knife at the back of the cutlery drawer, I shove it into the back of my jeans. My knife isn't going to do anything against a guy like Dominic, but I can't go into this without some way to protect myself.

Quickly glancing around my tiny apartment, I realize that I have everything I need to get out of here. My hand slams down on the kitchen counter, and I scoop up my car keys before grabbing my handbag and shoving it over my shoulder.

I turn for the door and run, leaving every light on and nothing but a mess behind. From now on, this apartment is no longer mine, and the name Veronica Davies will be left behind with it, just like I left Veronica Russo in Blaxlands Grove all those years ago.

Time for a new start, and hopefully, he'll never find me again.

My fingers curl around the door handle, and I yank it open, hauling all my shit behind me and struggling to get through the doorway.

As I step from the doorway, my eyes rise from the shitty carpet of my cheap apartment, and my heart explodes with fear. The lump forming in my throat making it nearly impossible to breathe.

Dominic Garcia.

He stands before me, dominating my doorway and leaving absolutely no hope of escape. His face twists into a devilish smirk, and the fear that pulses through my body cripples me.

He casually leans against my doorframe, looking me up and down with a gaze that burns right through to my soul. It's dangerous and deadly, filled with promises of misery. I instantly start backing up.

This can't be happening; I'm too late. I should have left all the clothes and the knife behind. I wasted my time, and now I'm screwed.

His eyes bore into mine. The more fear that appears on my face, the more his eyes seem to sparkle with excitement. He's been waiting for this, wanting and hoping, and for the first time since I was a confused and scared eighteen-year-old, he has me backed into a corner.

Nic takes a step into my apartment, never taking his heated gaze off mine. "Going somewhere?" he asks, his voice rumbling through my apartment, demanding attention. He takes another step and gives the door a shove, letting it slam closed with a BANG that vibrates right through my chest.

I try to swallow over the lump in my throat, taking another step back. "Get out," I snap, my hand uncurling from my suitcase before grabbing the knife in my back pocket.

He takes another daunting step toward me, and my hands begin to shake. "Now, now," he says with a tsk, amusement shining brightly in his eyes as though this is the best game he's ever played. He stalks toward me, and I back up until I slam against the wall with nowhere to run. "That's no way to greet an old friend," he taunts. "I've been waiting for this moment for a very long time."

My hand tightens around the knife, and as he pushes into me, I snap into survival mode. My hand whips out, and just as the blade springs free from the hilt, I slam it up against his throat. "Don't fucking touch me," I screech, watching as he freezes. "Leave now, and I'll forget this ever happened."

The corner of his lips pulls into a twisted smirk, the game getting that much more interesting for his sick little mind. "Or what? Whatcha' gonna' do, Roni?" he purrs, my name sitting on his lips like it was always supposed to be there. "Slit my throat? You don't have the fucking guts."

My jaw clenches, and as his body presses in closer, I smell that intoxicating scent from my teen years that got me into this trouble in the first place. The smell wraps around me, making it impossible to think clearly. "You don't know me, Nic," I tell him through my clenched jaw, spitting the words with hatred. "Not anymore. You have no idea what lengths I'd go to save myself and this life I've created."

He leans in closer, the blade pressing deeper against his skin and sending a drop of blood trailing down the thick column of his neck. "Then what are you waiting for? Do it, baby. Kill me and save yourself. This is your only shot. You're the only one I'd allow to get close enough."

My hands begin to shake as I start contemplating exactly what I have the strength to do. Sure, I could easily whip my hand out and end this right now, but could I live with myself afterward? I don't know. That's a question I'm not sure I'm capable of answering.

The seconds begin to tick by, and with each passing one, Nic's amusement only grows stronger. "Yeah," he says with a pathetic scoff, almost as though he's disappointed that I didn't take the bait. "That's what I thought. But don't worry, Roni. There's still time. I'll make you like me, I promise."

Then in the blink of an eye, Nic whips back from my blade and grabs my wrist, squeezing it so hard that I have no choice but to loosen my grip on the knife. His other hand shoots up and smacks the bottom of my hand, and the knife goes flying up into the sky.

He catches it with ease as my eyes bug out of my head.

I don't wait another second, especially now that he's armed.

I throw my handbag hard into his face, giving him a devastating shove into my shitty little kitchen before bolting for the door, this time not giving a shit about my suitcase.

My feet slam down against the flooring, pushing me faster and faster, and as my hand latches onto the door handle, I give it a hard yank, only it doesn't fucking budge.

I try again and again but get nowhere.

I glance back over my shoulder. The fucker must have locked it and taken the keys, but I don't have time to focus on it as he races toward me like a bull heading for his target, only this time, the amusement is gone.

The time for games is over.

I turn back to the door, desperately yanking on it before slamming my fists against the hardwood and hoping someone in this shitty little apartment complex might hear me. "HELP," I scream. "HELP ME."

A strong, thick, tattooed arm curls around my waist, and I'm yanked back from the door, his hand curling around my face and pressing against my mouth, muffling my screams. "I really hoped we could do this the easy way," he tells me, walking back toward my living room, only to smirk at the image of his mugshot still on my television screen.

I'm just about to tell him exactly what I think of his 'easy way' when I feel pressure against the side of my neck, and within seconds, my world fades to black.

CHAPTER 2
DOMINIC

Wind whips through the open window of Sebastian's beat-up car as I race down the highway, desperately trying to distance myself from Bellevue Springs. Every cop in the fucking area is swarming the streets looking for me, but I'm not here to make their job easy. I'm going to make it fucking impossible.

The phone Kairo gave me after we ditched the transport van on the side of the highway screeches through the quiet car, and I glance down at it to find Sebastian's name across the screen.

A grin pulls at my lips as I hit accept and bring the phone to my ear while rolling up the old window. "Sup, bro?"

"Dude, I don't give a fuck that you've just spent six years locked up. Bring my fucking car back and pick our asses up. We ain't walking all the way back to Breakers. There're fucking cops everywhere."

"Go say hi then," I taunt, more than desperate to teach those fuckers a lesson after keeping Ocean's baby girl Storm a secret from me for the past three years. "I'm sure they're all dying to chat with you. Maybe let them know what you've been up to today. I'm sure they'd love to hear all about it."

"Fuck off, man," he says with a pissed off grunt, proving that after six and a half years away, my crew still ain't going to let me get away with shit. "Where are you?"

"Halfway home," I tell him.

"Kai hasn't prepped the Widows," he says with a strange hesitation in his tone. "They don't know you're coming home and taking over."

"Taking over? I'm not fucking taking over," I say with a scoff. "I'm taking back what's already mine. Kai was only stepping in, and they fucking know that. I'm the real leader here, don't forget it. As for the Widows, my face is on every fucking TV screen across the country. If those fuckers haven't figured out that I'm coming home to raise my fucking army, then they shouldn't be wearing the Black Widow mark."

"Good point," he grumbles, hating being put in his place, proving again that some things will never change, no matter how hard you try. "So," he continues. "Where are we on the lift home?"

I roll my eyes, a grin pulling at the side of my mouth. "Ocean has a whole fucking garage filled with cars. I'm sure she'll lend you dickheads one for the day."

Sebastian scoffs and I hear him relaying my solution to the boys, only to hear two more scoffs. "Really?" Sebastian finally says. "Because three Widows rolling around Bellevue Springs in a fucking Bentley won't look suspicious at all."

"Not my problem, man," I laugh. "But thanks for the ride."

With that, I end the call, knowing that I'll be hearing about it when they get back into Breakers Flats, but as I said, it's not my fucking problem. They're big boys now. They can take care of themselves, just as they've been doing for the last six and a half years. They don't need me anymore, they learned to adapt, learned to survive without me, but fuck knows I need them more than ever before.

Kairo, Elijah, and Sebastian are my crew. They've had my back through thick and thin, even when I was at my worst. They've always looked out for me just as I've done the same for them, even when I nearly destroyed the one thing that mattered to us all—Oceania Munroe. That's all in the past now, and I like to think that we're all in a better place. That was until I found out that she hid her kid from me, but I guess that's on the boys as well.

Seeing that little girl hit me out of nowhere. I wasn't expecting it at all, but the more I think about it, the more I start putting the pieces together. There were four months a few years back when Ocean didn't visit me at all, claiming she had things going on. She'd call instead, so I didn't think much of it. She could have easily hidden the early stages of her pregnancy under baggy clothes, but there comes a time where a woman just can't hide it. I guess that's when she stopped coming to visit. But why though? It doesn't make sense.

Not wanting to fuck things up for her now, especially since she has a kid and a wedding to organize, I'll be reserving this discussion for the boys. As much as I adore that girl, now that I'm out, she needs to know that I'm not going to make her life a living hell. Things are going to be different now. I need to steer clear, at least for a little while. Though, that doesn't mean that I won't be making someone else's life a living hell.

That thought has another grin stretching wide over my face as I roll the window back down and relax into the driver's seat. It's a long drive back to Breakers Flats, so I sure hope little Roni Russo is comfortable in the trunk back there.

She's such a fucking firecracker. She always has been, thinking that she's stronger than what she is. Her dickhead brother let her believe that when she was a kid and it was the biggest mistake he ever made. Sometimes being honest with yourself is a lot safer than pretending you're not scared. She puts on a brave face when deep down, she's never been so terrified. Especially when it comes to me.

Roni used to be my girl back in high school. She was the first chick I ever gave myself to, but because our fathers were the leaders of opposing gangs, it was impossible. Not a soul knew about us, but now that Russo is gone and I'm in fucking charge, things will be changing. Veronica Russo won't be hiding from me anymore. As of now, she's mine.

The next few weeks will be interesting though, not only am I going to have to deal with Roni, but I'll be figuring out how to get myself back on top without my dumb ass getting arrested and thrown back in prison. Hell, I might even have to start going by an alias to keep myself hidden. Getting back on top is going to be the hardest thing I'll ever do, especially with Christian Russo leading the Wolves, but my men are loyal. They'll follow me to the ends of the earth.

I get thirty minutes out from Breakers Flats—completely lost in my thoughts of exactly how I'm going to play this—when a loud banging comes from the trunk.

A wide, excited smile stretches across my face.

It's fucking showtime.

Pissed off groans and grunts come from the trunk before I hear her kicking against the back seat of the car in desperation. But she won't be getting out of there, not until I allow her.

The banging only gets louder, and I can't help but call out. "Everything alright back there?"

"FUCK YOU, DOMINIC GARCIA. YOU CAN SUCK MY DICK. I HATE YOU."

Fuck, I love it when she talks dirty. It's like being pulled straight back to high school. It's not the first time she's told me to suck her dick and I'm sure as fuck that it won't be the last. Though, a chick like Roni; if she actually had one, I'm sure it'd be fucking huge.

I yank hard on the steering wheel and pull into the next lane, chuckling as I hear her tumbling around in the back. "What was that, baby? I didn't quite hear you."

"FUCK YOU." Her screech comes out in a high-pitched squeal that I don't think I've ever heard another human make before. Is that shit even natural? "LET ME OUT OF THIS GODDAMN TRUNK."

"No can do, baby," I tell her. "But don't worry. I won't keep you locked up in there much longer."

"You're a fucking sick psychopath, Dominic. You need therapy."

There's a loud bang against the backseat, and I can't help but glance up in the rearview mirror, double-checking that she didn't get herself free. I wouldn't put it past her; she's always managed to evade me. Why should now be any different? Seeing that she didn't get far, I focus back on the highway. "Did your fancy psychology degree tell you that? Or are you going off personal experience?"

"Both," she grunts before four more loud bangs and thumps echo through the car. "Christian is going to kill you for this," she snaps. "Just wait until he gets his hands on you."

I laugh, letting her hear the sinister tone in my voice. "And how's he even going to know? Tell me, baby, when was the last time you called him? I know I sure as shit haven't spoken to him recently."

She falls quiet. She knows I'm right. He may be the leader of the Wolves, and sure, I'll give the fucker credit, he's turned all their bullshit around, but he'll never get his hands on me. Hell, the only way anyone is ever going to find out about this is through me, and I'll be keeping this little secret on the down-low.

No more screeches, protests, or loathing comes from the trunk, and as I listen to the muffled noises of her trying to break free, I can't help but think back on her brother.

Christian Russo is a dick, yet despite being the leader of the Wolves and stepping right into his father's tainted footsteps, I can't find it in me to hate him. He did what anyone of us would have done, and he did it while somehow making himself out to be some kind of hero.

I knew shit was going to hit the fucking fan the second Ocean handed over the leadership to Christian. She trusted him blindly, and while she should have trusted me instead, I can't seem to fault her.

I know her better than she knows herself, at least, I used to. Which is how I knew she was going to hand over the leadership to Christian before she even knew it herself. While it was the best decision for her to make, she couldn't have known the kind of bullshit that would bring down over me. I did, though, and I was fucking prepared. It's the reason I allowed myself to get arrested and put behind bars for ten fucking years.

When Christian officially took over, the Wolves wanted to turn on him. Every fucker in there thought that they deserved the leadership, which is how I ended up with a fucking target on my head. Take me out, and they get to be the hero. Christian could have saved us all the fucking drama just by admitting that he was Russo's biological son, but he had to go and prove himself instead. He wanted to earn it just like the rest of the fuckers did. Fuck, I've never been so happy that Ocean was able to distance herself from that bullshit and start fresh with her douchebag, rich prick of a boyfriend.

The number of Wolves inside that prison that came for my fucking head was insane. Every. Fucking. Day. Threat after threat until they finally realized that no one was going to bring me down. I'm Dominic Fucking Garcia; if you want to take me out, then you better bring the whole fucking cavalry.

I pull into an abandoned lot and look over the old warehouse that my father won in a bet over twenty years ago and let out a sigh. It's a complete run-down piece of shit and will probably fall to the fucking ground during the next storm. But until I can find something more suitable to keep me hidden from the rest of the world while I run the Widows, this is home.

My father never put his name on this property, and it's never been connected to the Widows. The police will never find me here, and neither will my enemies. Kai, Eli, and Sebastian are the only ones who know that I'm here, and they're the only ones I'd ever trust with that information. After all, if they give me up to the cops, they're coming right along with me for breaking me out in the first place. One of us goes down, we all go down. That's just how it's always been.

There's an underground bunker beneath it, which is where I'll be staying for the foreseeable future. I drive right around the warehouse and through the back garage door, looking around to make sure none of the neighboring warehouses have eyes on me. Though what would it matter if they did? If someone was to squeal around here, they'd end up with a bullet between their eyes. People in Breakers Flats know to keep to themselves. It's the only way to survive around here.

I bring the car to a stop right beside the piece of shit car the boys got for me to use, knowing that the second they show up here later tonight, Sebastian will be taking it right back.

Getting out of the car, I make my way around to the backseat and grab the suitcase Roni packed and the handbag she'd thrown in my face. She probably won't be needing that for a while, but she went to the effort of bringing it with her when she wanted to run, so I figured why the hell not?

I stash all her shit at the hidden entrance of the underground bunker, and as I turn to go back for Roni and look over the back of the car, I can't help but smile to myself. The fucking smartass has kicked out the taillight and has probably spent the last half hour waving down passing cars, trying to get help. But what's more, the little princess is watching me through the small hole, and with her eyes on me, I feel like I could do anything. Though, that also means that she knows exactly where she is.

I make my way toward her and watch her eyes narrow into slits with every step I take. My girl isn't afraid; she's pissed.

I pop the trunk, and she immediately tries to fly out of it, coming at me with a force I didn't realize she was capable of. She must have taken self-defense lessons or at least logged a few hours in the gym every day. I wouldn't be surprised, she looks fucking good, but no amount of hours in a gym is a match for me.

I catch her with ease, pushing her back before she tumbles right out of the trunk and hurts herself. "Go to hell," she growls, looking at me with nothing but pure hatred.

I lean in, reaching down and lowering my face to hers, watching as her eyes fill with uncertainty. As my nose brushes across her skin, she sucks in a sharp breath that tells me exactly what I already know. She may have run from me for all these years, but I never lost her. She's always been mine. That's the pact we made in high school, and I intend to hold her to it.

My hands slip around her toned waist, and as my eyes come back to hers, I can't help but grin down at her, my lips only an inch away.

"Gladly, but you're coming with me."

With that, I haul her out of the trunk of Sebastian's beat-up car and turn on my heel. Roni struggles over my shoulder, kicking and screaming as we approach the door to our little underground bunker. No one can hear her out here, and the thought brings a laugh rumbling through my chest.

My hand smacks down over her firm ass, holding her still so that she doesn't fall. "Welcome home, baby."

CHAPTER 3

RONI

Nic throws me down on a shitty little bed that feels like it was made out of concrete, and I stare at him in horror. What the fuck is this? Is this the moment that I'm going to be tied up and used as his personal sex slave?

I've been working as a therapist and a guidance counselor for nearly eight years. While I've never met someone who's been used as a sex slave, I've certainly talked to girls who have suffered at the hands of rape, and I don't know if I'm strong enough to make it out the other end if that were to happen.

"Don't fucking look at me like that," Nic snaps in disgust, turning away and walking back to the door to grab my suitcase and handbag.

"Who the fuck do you think I am?"

I scoff, unable to keep the accusatory, sarcastic tone out of my voice. "Is that supposed to be a trick question, or do I need to remind you that you broke out of prison less than four hours ago? You're a fucking murderer. You killed my father and my boyfriend. Your rap sheet is a million pages long, and you have no issue barging into my home, knocking me the fuck out, shoving my ass in a trunk, and kidnapping me. So, you tell me, is rape something I need to be prepared for? Because I honestly don't know anymore."

Nic glares at me, his jaw clenched as anger pours through his eyes, but he can't deny that I'm right. "You better watch your fucking tone," he snaps, striding toward me and making me catch my breath. He grabs my shoulders and throws me back on the bed, coming down over me so that his face hovers just above mine. "When I fuck you, it'll be because you fucking begged me for it. Because it's the only thing you can think about, because you craved it, needed it so fucking bad that you couldn't even think straight. You're going to be screaming for more and loving it. Is that clear? I might have done some fucked-up bullshit over the years, but I'm no rapist and you fucking know it."

I swallow over the lump in my throat, unable to respond. Not because I don't know it, but because any sound that comes out of my mouth is going to give away the fact that his closeness already has my body screaming for him. That's a whole can of beans I'm not prepared to spill just yet.

Nic's dark, haunting eyes narrow, not moving an inch from mine as he breathes heavily, almost as though our closeness is affecting him just as much as it affects me. "I said, is that fucking clear?" he growls, not prepared to let it go unanswered.

I give him a short, sharp nod and finally take a breath of relief as he pulls back from me, taking that intoxicating scent with him.

He's a fucking maniac. I should be terrified. I should be searching the room for a way out, but instead, I'm too busy focusing on him. He's the definition of toxic, and I shouldn't be so attracted to it. Something has got to be wrong with me. Maybe I was wired wrong or dropped on my head as a baby because this is some seriously messed up shit.

Nic takes a look around what I assume is his new home on his way back to the door. He pulls it open and grabs my bag before hauling it inside and dumping it on the dirty floor of the bunker. I watch him through a sharp gaze, studying his every movement, still fearing for my life.

What the hell is this? Does he think I'm just going to stay here while he hides from the law as some kind of house bitch? Fuck that. I'll be out of here the second he turns his back. I won't let him pull me down like he did in high school.

Nic is like a black hole, constantly pulling me toward him and tempting me with what's inside, but if I'm not careful, I'll get sucked in and never return again. I'm not sure if he realized this, but I'm pretty damn fond of the life I've been fortunate enough to build for myself, and this bullshit is really fucking with that. Hell, after all of this is said and done, I'll be the one needing therapy.

I adjust myself on the stiff bed to a position that makes it easier to run and watch every step he takes. He walks around the small, dusty bunker with the cheap light above his head, slowly rocking back and forth like some kind of horror film.

He starts searching through cupboards and having a good look around, and it dawns on me that he hasn't been here before. At least, not in the last six and a half years since he's been locked away. He has no idea what supplies are in here or what he may or may not need to survive. Hell, is there even any food down here, or does he plan on giving away his location every time he calls for pizza?

He's screwed. It's only a matter of time before someone finds him, and he goes back to where he belongs. I just have to keep breathing until that happens.

He walks past the shitty bed and opens a door into a narrow bathroom, and to be honest, I'm shocked that this place comes equipped with basic human amenities. I don't know what I expected; maybe a bucket. I peer around him, trying to search the bathroom from my awkward position on the bed for a window to escape through. I'm not that lucky, though. Nic was probably prepared for this.

Realizing that I'm completely screwed, I lean back against the wall, crossing my arms over my chest. A small huff comes tearing out of me and my eyes go wide. I hadn't meant to make a sound. Now all I've done is drawn even more attention to myself.

My eyes snap up to Nic as his back stiffens.

Fuck. Not good.

He takes a step out of the small bathroom and turns his ferocious glare on me, his gaze sharp and deadly. "Is there something you need to say?" he demands, not coming any closer, but even having him near the bathroom door is still far too close.

Figuring that I have nothing to lose, I raise my chin and decide that I won't be going down without a fight. I climb off the bed and stand in the middle of the room, showing him that I'm not scared of his bullshit, despite the fear that's rapidly pulsing through my veins. "What is this?" I demand, turning up my nose to the shitty little bunker as though I'm too good to be living in filth like this, but truth be told, in my escape from the Wolves, I lived in much worse conditions before I could get back on my feet. "Do you expect me to just sit around your shitty little bunker every day being some deranged housewife? I'm Veronica Fucking Russo. My brother is going to kill you when he finds out what you did."

Nic scoffs. "Let Christian come," he booms as though it's the funniest thing he's ever heard. "I've been meaning to have a little catch up with him."

My blood runs cold as I take his words for exactly what they are; a threat. "If you even think about hurting my brother, I'll—"

"You'll what?" he says, moving forward like a predator stalking his prey, his eyes taunting and laughing at me. He steps right into me, his tall frame looming over mine, yet somehow I manage to stand my ground. "What could you possibly do to stop me? Run to daddy like you used to in high school? Oh, wait …"

Low fucking blow.

My jaw clenches, and without hesitation, I slam my knee up into his junk. But without even flinching or taking his stormy eyes from mine, his hands connect with my knee just moments before impact.

He clutches my knee, his fingers digging into my skin, and making me wobble on one foot. "That's really how you want to play this?" he questions, leaning into me and somehow keeping me upright with his awkward hold, saving me from falling flat on my ass.

I grab hold of his large, strong shoulder and use it as leverage to yank my knee out of his tight grip. "Look around you, Nic. You're the one who started this bullshit game. I'm just finishing it."

He laughs, and the sound not only wraps around me like a warm blanket but pierces right through to my soul. "Baby, you ain't finishing shit. I say when this is over."

I scoff, raising a brow at his cocky demeanor. "It's not a game if only one of us is playing."

Nic leans into me again, his big hand curling around my waist and pulling me in against his strong, ripped body. My hand instinctively falls against his chest. "The Roni I remember used to love playing games."

I raise my chin. "The Roni you remember doesn't exist anymore. I've changed. I'm not the pathetic girl who would have followed you to the ends of the earth. She's gone."

He shakes his head, the corner of his lips lifting into a devastatingly sexy smirk as though he's actually enjoying this bullshit. "No, baby. That Roni is still in there. I can feel her dying to break free."

I narrow my gaze, and just as I'm about to tell him to get fucked, the sound of a car screeching through the warehouse has his back stiffening and his eyes flicking to the door. He releases me in seconds. "Stay here," he orders, his tone low and terrifying, filled with authority.

He walks through the small bunker, stopping by a cupboard and pulling out a gun. I watch him with wide eyes, cowering in the bunker as he reaches the door. He peeks out, and with a sigh of relief, pushes through to the dark warehouse.

"Where the fuck have you bastards been?" he calls.

Shit. He knows these guys.

The door slams shut behind him, but my curiosity has me moving through the bunker. I walk up the concrete steps to the door and reach for the handle before taking a shaky breath. I can hear their muffled conversation, but hearing isn't as good as seeing, especially when I have absolutely no idea what the fuck is going on.

I gently twist the handle, willing the door to open without making a sound. It peels back, and I have to shuffle around, but I keep it closed enough not to draw attention to myself. I watch as Nic makes his way over to a car that looks as though it belongs in places like Bellevue Springs rather than this shithole.

Three guys pour out of the vehicle, and immediately it's obvious it doesn't belong to them. They're Widows, and judging by the fact that they knew exactly where to find Nic, they're important. I wonder if these are the three friends Ocean had told me about; Kairo, Sebastian, and Elijah.

I've done my best to keep away from the Widows and Wolves, but news of Kairo taking over while Nic was incarcerated spread far and wide. I just wish I could put a face to the name. I've never met them before, and right now, I don't know if that's a good or bad thing. Ocean speaks about them as though they're the best guys in the world, but looking at them now, they look like they just stepped straight out of hell. These aren't the kind of guys who should be fucked with.

The three men fall around Nic, pulling him into a warm hug, clapping him on the back, and congratulating him for getting this far. They talk and laugh, completely oblivious to the fact that he brought home a stray.

It only takes a few minutes for the boys to get past their bullshit and get serious. They start taking Nic around the warehouse, showing him where they've stored everything that he'll need to survive in here. They take him through a security system that's complete with surveillance, making it that much harder for me to escape. But my interest is piqued when the taller guy in the center looks Nic dead in the eyes and says, "Alright, your weapons are over here."

I watch with a keen eye as they cut across the warehouse, but I don't miss the way Nic's gaze sweeps back to the door and finds me watching. His eyes narrow, and I know he's silently telling me to mind my own damn business, but like hell that will be happening. If there are weapons in this place, then I want to know exactly how to get my hands on them.

Not wanting to give me away, Nic focuses back on his friends, and I gape in horror as a large metal door is pulled open, revealing more weapons than I've ever seen in my life. It's as though these guys had raided the evidence locker of the Breakers Flats police department. There's enough shit in here to sink the whole fucking country which makes it clear that the Widows haven't just been surviving while Nic was gone, but they've been thriving.

The Wolves would never be able to stand against weapons like that. I don't know what Christian and his men have been up to over the past few years, but I do know if he had any idea what kind of arsenal the Widows have hidden, it'd be a war.

There is no way in hell I want to stick around long enough to see how this plays out.

I have a life back home, I have a job that I love, and patients who come to me for peace of mind. I can't just step away from that to play the role of a gangster's chew toy.

I have to get out of here.

Closing the door as gently as I can, I pull back, not wanting to get caught by the other guys. It's one thing for Nic to have me hidden away in here, but having those guys find me … nope. Hell to the motherfucking nope. I don't know them, don't know if they're good or bad. I can't just take Ocean's word for it. Who knows if these are even the same guys she knows. These could be random dickheads Nic met in prison. It's not a risk I'm willing to take.

Feeling the helplessness wash over me, I drop to the step, my ass hitting it far too hard, but what does it matter? It's not like I'm going to live through this. If I try to run, Nic will kill me, and if I hang around, he'll play with me first and then try to kill me.

They're not great options.

Fuck it. If I'm going to die anyway, then it'll be before some dickhead gets the chance to destroy me first.

I fly up off the concrete step and start searching through the bunker. Nic had found a gun earlier as easily as opening a cupboard and reaching in. Surely there must be more than just one hiding out in here.

I start with the little kitchen, yanking open the drawers and madly searching each of them. I find a small knife but it won't help me. Using a knife means I have to get close to him, and I can't risk that. He'll overpower me within seconds. I could always throw it at him but knowing Nic, he'll just shrug off a stab wound like he was swatting a fly. I shove it in the back pocket of my jeans anyway. I'm sure I'll need it at some point.

The kitchen comes up empty, and I hurry over to the dresser in the adjoining bedroom. Desperately searching through the drawers, I toss piles of clothes to the floor, leaving every one of them open as I go. But when I pull out the top drawer, the whole dresser becomes unbalanced and crashes to the concrete floor.

FUCK!

My eyes go wide, and I become frantic, searching for something to protect myself.

Without a doubt, they heard me, and they're coming to check what the fuck is going on in here.

As if on cue, I hear the boys rushing toward the bunker, their feet slamming against the concrete and echoing throughout the warehouse. I rush to the door and slide the lock into place, knowing damn well that it's not going to stop them, but it will at least give me a few seconds.

The door violently rattles as I rush around the bunker, still pulling open drawers and cupboards. Just as I yank the couch away from the wall, I find a gun taped to the back, and the door flies open with an inhuman force.

The four Widows storm the bunker, and I dive for the gun, desperately reaching. My fingers curl around the cool metal, but I can't get a good grip before Nic hauls me up and slams me roughly against the wall.

"I thought we'd already learned this lesson," he growls, his voice deep and menacing as he reaches around me, curling his hand around my ass and yanking the knife out of my back pocket.

"Fuck you," I snap, fighting against his hold.

"Yo," one of the guys says, cautiously walking toward us while glancing back at his friends. "What the fuck is going on here? Who is this? We never discussed hostages."

Nic glares back at his friend. "Get the fuck out of here. This is between me and her. It has nothing to do with you guys or the Widows. It's personal."

The Widows glance between one another, and it's clear that whatever the fuck is going on here wasn't part of anyone's plans. But they're not about to do anything about it, either. The taller guy steps forward, his eyes on me. "Is that Veronica Russo?"

Nic turns on his friends, keeping me hidden behind his large frame. "I said get the fuck out of here."

He shakes his head while the other two retreat, clearly not liking this turn of events. "Ocean's going to fucking kill you, man," the guy says, making me wonder if this is Kairo, the one not afraid to stand up against Nic. "You know they're friends."

"What O doesn't know won't hurt her," Nic says, his voice filled with regret, knowing his friend is right. I've heard all about Nic's relationship with Ocean, and at first, it made me jealous as all hell, but I quickly saw how wrong and toxic it was. What they had wasn't love; it was comfort. But what we had back in high school … shit. That was the fucking world.

The Widow shakes his head. "Can't do that, bro."

Nic nods, giving into his friend easily and making me wonder about the depth and complexity of their friendship. "Do what you have to do," Nic tells him, "But you know just as well as I do that she's going to try and swoop in to save the day. She's got a kid and a wedding to worry about. She doesn't need to be getting mixed up in this world again. If she gets hurt, that's on you."

The guy drops his gaze as the others hover by the door. "Alright," he finally says. "I won't say shit, but if you hurt her," he adds. "You'll have me to deal with. We're not about to start a war with the Wolves over this bullshit."

Nic scoffs. "A war with the Wolves is coming whether you like it or not." He throws his heavy gaze back at me. "As for her, she'll be fine as long as she behaves." I meet his eyes and as he watches me, I can't help but feel that he's being honest. He doesn't want to hurt me, and while that should ease my fears, it doesn't. I still have to get out of here and run as far and wide as I can.

All four of the guys send their heavy stares my way, and I swallow back fear. I've never experienced anything quite so intense, but one by one, they make their way out of the bunker until it's just me and Nic standing in awkward silence.

We listen as the stolen car screeches out of the warehouse until it's just us, finally alone. Nic seems to relax, and I watch as he moves across the trashed bunker, picking up random things and placing them back on shelves. "Are you just going to stand there or clean up this shit?"

I don't respond, more than content to stand and watch.

He shrugs his shoulders. "Fine by me," he says, walking back out the door and returning later with Chinese takeout containers. "Hungry?"

All I can do is stare as he drops the food on the counter and starts digging in.

What the fuck is this? He's acting like we're just chilling out, about to put on a movie and snuggle on the fucking couch. Is he insane? Actually, that's a question I'm not sure I want answered.

"If you're not going to eat, you might as well go to bed. It's getting late."

"Bed?" I scoff. "Do you really think I'm stupid enough to fall asleep around you?"

"Suit yourself," he says, grabbing the takeout container and dropping down onto the chair at the shitty little table.

With nothing else to do and nowhere to go, I walk right over to the opposite side of the bunker and drop down onto the old, dirty couch, thankful that he hasn't chained me up or hurt me. Maybe he really did mean it; maybe he hasn't dragged me here to kill me after all. Maybe there's something much, much worse in my future.

CHAPTER 4
DOMINIC

Silence pulses through the cold bunker as I look up at the ceiling, not seeing a damn thing in the darkness, but it's nothing new to me. I've done nothing but live in darkness for the past six and a half years. I'll take this bunker over the bullshit I went through any day.

I crashed into bed the second my Chinese takeout had gone down. Something is just so soothing about being able to lie down without the threat of my cellmate suffocating me during the night, not that he could have. He was a pussy, even if he had ties to the Wolves. He fucking tried time and time again to take me out, but he never got far enough to cause any real damage. The fucker quickly learned not to touch me.

Good times.

My eyes begin to grow heavy. I can't wait to get a good night's sleep for the first time in six years. I could sleep for a fucking week straight and still need more. Don't get me wrong, I fucking flourished in prison. Every fucker in there was at my beck and call while having the outside world terrified for my release, knowing that the second I got out, I was going to rise to the fucking top. Anything I wanted in there was mine. A joint? Done. A phone? Done. A fucking bitch to suck my cock? As easy as clicking my fucking fingers. Not even prison could stop the leader of the Black Widows. I even had guards falling at my feet and begging for favors; that's part of the reason why escaping was even possible.

But being here—away from all that bullshit and with Roni in my sights—I can finally breathe again. It's time to take my place as the rightful leader and show the world that the Black Widows are the most feared and lethal motherfuckers around. We're going to rise to the top and put down all the other bastards who even try to touch us, and what's more, I'm taking Roni along for the ride.

Thinking that I'm asleep, I hear her get up from her position on the far side of the couch. She's been sitting in that same spot for three hours. It's well after midnight, so she must be fucking tired, but sleep won't be coming easy for her, not tonight at least. I'm not so much of a monster that I can't see that she's freaking out. She's fucking terrified. She doesn't know what's happening, where she's going to end up, or what I even have planned for her, but she shouldn't fear. I was telling her the truth when I said that I wasn't going to hurt her. I just need to keep her around for a little while, and if she still insists that she's not the same girl I used to love, then I'll let her go. But if she realizes what I already know to be true—then I'm taking my girl back and never letting her go.

She creeps across the bunker, and I hear her pause as the ground creeks beneath her. I can almost feel her eyes on me, making sure that she hasn't 'woken' me. She takes a relieved breath when I don't move and continues her way through the kitchen. She rummages around in the cutlery drawer, and I grin to myself as I hear her pick up the Chinese takeout container that I'd left for her. I fucking knew she was hungry, but I also knew that she was way too stubborn to accept the food that I offered.

There's a light squeal of the chair being dragged back from the dining table before she drops into it, seeming a little less concerned about waking me.

I listen as she practically forces the food down her throat as fast as possible in her rush to get back to what she's deemed as her side of the bunker. I can't help but laugh and have to cover it up as a light snore so that I don't alarm her. If she knew I was awake, she'd freak the fuck out and race over to the couch, leaving her dinner behind. With what I have planned for her, she's going to need as much energy as she can get.

Before I know it, I hear the sound of the fork scraping along the bottom of the container. It's placed down on the table, and just to be an ass, she leaves it there for me to clean up. Roni takes herself back over to the couch, and I listen as she lowers herself back into it.

My eyes grow heavy, and feeling content that she's not going to starve, I allow myself to finally go to sleep, knowing that at some point, she'll find the courage to sleep too.

Memories of my time in prison come swarming through my dreams, visions of the men I've killed, strangled, beaten. Every last one is on a constant loop every time I close my eyes, a reminder of the terrible things I've done under the name of the Widows.

A familiar, soft click has my eyes snapping open and consciousness rushing back to me. My arm shoots out, my hand curling around the cool metal of the gun and pushing it away just moments before the bullet flies straight past my fucking head.

I stare up at Roni with tears in her eyes, looking horrified at what she just tried to do, but I don't fucking blame her. If I were in her position, I would too. We stare at each other for a silent moment, my ears ringing from the shot, both our hearts racing.

I should have known that she would try something. The Roni that I knew was a fighter. She would never have just given up and let me play my twisted little games. That's on me for turning my back, for assuming that she was just going to sit back and accept her fate. When in reality, if any of the fuckers in my life are equal to me, it's her. She just doesn't know it yet, but I'll show her in time.

Roni starts to shake her head, fear shining in her eyes, not knowing how I'll react. "I ... I ..."

My heart fucking breaks for her. This life isn't an easy one, especially after being away from it for so long. I doubt she's ever shot anyone before, and having me as her first target only proves that she has balls made of steel.

"Shhhh," I soothe, tugging on the gun that's still firmly in her hand. I pull her hard into me, and she collapses down on the bed. "It's okay," I tell her, wrapping her in my arms and feeling her head resting against my chest as her tears begin staining my shirt. "It's not the first time a beautiful woman has tried to kill me in my sleep."

"I just …" sob, "wasn't thinking. I found the … the gun, and the next thing I knew, it was in my hand, and I just … went for it."

Fuck. Kairo and his stupid fucking guns. They're all over the place. He wanted me to be prepared, not knowing what kind of bullshit was going to rain down over me, but just how many fucking guns did he stash in here? I've already got the one from the cupboard and from behind the couch. Now, this? How many more do I need to know about? There's already a whole fucking stash out in the warehouse.

"It's okay," I tell her, my hand roaming up and down her back as I stare up at the ceiling for the second time tonight, only this time it's as I catch my breath after my whole fucking life flashed before my eyes.

Roni shakes her head against my chest. "It's not okay," she insists, her sobs still coming in hard and fast. "I tried to kill you. Kill, Nic. This isn't just some stupid game. I nearly took your life, and I'm so fucking tired that I didn't even think about it. Just pointed and shot." She grabs my shirt and attempts to wipe her eyes. "I mean, fuck. I was in love with you for fucking years. What kind of person does that? Who shoots a man they were in love with? I'm a monster, and now you're going to kill me because I almost put a bullet through your head."

"Baby," I laugh, pulling her in tighter and absolutely loving the feel of having her in my arms again. I mean, yeah, she's been in my arms plenty of times over the past twelve hours but she was either passed out or desperately trying to get away, so they don't count. Right now, though, she's here, letting me hold her and seeking out my comfort, and that means more than she'll ever know. "I could never kill you, Roni. Not even if you put that bullet through my head, but that doesn't mean your bullshit isn't going to go unpunished."

Her eyes go wide, and she raises onto her elbow to look down at me. Fear takes over as she searches my eyes for some kind of answer. "No," she begs. "Whatever it is, don't make me do it. I swear I won't try and hurt you again. I was just … so tired. I wanted to go home, back to my life, and pretend that none of this ever happened."

I pull her back to me, and she comes without hesitation. "That's not going to happen," I tell her. "Try it again, though, and your sweet ass will be locked in chains. Is that clear?"

Roni nods, her eyes coming back to meet mine. "What are you going to do to me?" she questions, her hand falling back to my chest and her fingers tangling into the fabric of my shirt just like she used to do back in high school. Memories of all our good times together fly through my mind, and while I know I did things in a twisted way, I know I'm right. She needs to be here with me.

I shake my head, bringing my hand down to her face and running my knuckles over her porcelain skin. She leans into my touch, and her eyes flutter with need. "Sleep, Roni," I tell her, unable to get the vision of her standing above me with that gun out of my head. "We can discuss it in the morning."

She falls silent beside me, and I wonder if she's plotting her escape when her breathing softens, and she becomes heavy in my arms, finally falling into a deep sleep. I pull her in tighter and she instantly snuggles into me, her leg hitching high over my hip.

My hand falls to her thigh, and as I bask in the feel of her body against mine for the first time in years, I realize that while she may hate every little thing about me, she still trusts me to keep her safe. A woman who didn't would never fall asleep in the arms of a killer, it's just common sense, but Roni … she's different. She's strong, fierce, and has the potential to rule it all. She just has to figure it out.

Feeling content for the first time in over ten years, I finally close my eyes and let unconsciousness claim me. Tomorrow, things are going to be different.

My body wakes me at the crack of dawn, just as it's been trained to do during my time in prison. It takes me a moment to remember that I'm not back there, and from here on out, things are going to change.

Roni stirs in my arms, and I glance down at her. I've woken up beside many women, but never have any looked so damn peaceful. If only she knew what kind of power she holds over me. She always has, and I'm sick of holding it back.

It won't be long, and she'll slot straight back into my life just as she's always meant to be.

I slip out of her arms, and it kills me. I'd do anything to spend the day wrapped in her body. Fuck knows it's been a long time since I slipped inside a woman like this and fucked her until she was seeing stars. If things go my way, she'll be the only woman I'll ever fuck again, but if it doesn't, I'll make sure that no other bastard gets a taste of what's mine.

Fuck, what I wouldn't do to roll her onto her back, spread those pretty thighs, and taste her again. But there's shit to get done, an empire to rebuild, and a fucking traitor to slaughter.

When your title comes as the leader of the Black Widows, work is never done, not even when you're locked behind bars. I hear the familiar sound of a car pulling into the warehouse, and I pause for a moment, making sure it's the sound that I'm expecting and not of an enemy already finding me. It's only been one day since breaking out of that godforsaken prison, and there's no way in hell that I'm going back yet. I'll be dead before my ass is dragged back there, though there's also a very real possibility that if this is an enemy, my death could be the goal.

It ain't gonna happen. Not on my watch, and definitely not with Roni here.

The car comes to a screeching halt, and my hand automatically falls to the gun at my back. I pull it out from the waistband of my pants and creep toward the door until I hear car doors opening and Sebastian's familiar grunt.

I let out a sigh of relief then listen to a scuffle followed by the sound of flesh being beaten on. There's a loud thump, three-car doors slamming, and then tires screeching on the warehouse floors before screeching right back out.

I don't bother going to check on the package that was just delivered. I trust my boys. I know that my delivery is right where I want it and left in a state that makes playing mind games all that much more fun. Though unfortunately for me, the fun is going to have to wait until sleeping beauty here wakes. After all, she held a gun to my head while I slept and decided to pull the trigger. Despite how I feel about her, a crime like that will not go unpunished.

CHAPTER 5

RONI

The sound of huffing pulls me from a deep sleep, and it takes a moment for me to register where I am. The past twenty-four hours have been hell, but I slept like a baby in Nic's arms. Now that the memories are rushing back, I feel like a complete idiot.

How could I have been so stupid? Not only did I try to shoot the dickhead in his sleep, but I climbed in bed with him and cried on his chest as though he wasn't a dangerous, psychotic, escaped criminal.

I'm not just an idiot; I'm a complete fool. He could have slit my throat while I slept or taken advantage of me. God, what was I thinking?

My stare instantly lands on Nic as he sits across the bunker on the couch. I had only just claimed it as mine last night, though considering I took over his bed, I guess it's only fair.

His lethal gaze is already on mine and judging by the scowl that accompanies it, I'd dare say that someone is a little sour that he's had to wait for me to wake, but seriously? What is this? I was just kidnapped from my home. Why bother waiting until I wake for whatever deranged plan he has for me today. He could have just dragged me out of bed by my ankle, which would have been a massive step up to the way he dragged me out of my apartment.

My glare sharpens. "What?" I snap, hating the way that he's watching me with a gaze that could not only tear me apart but one that could set my body on fire in all the best ways.

Nic rolls his eyes as though my snappy attitude is beneath him. He clambers off the couch and checks his gun. "Get up," he orders, tearing his stare off mine and ripping something right out of my chest as he does.

I struggle to catch a breath as he gets up and disregards me as though I'm nothing. Why does that hurt so much? He held me through the night, even though I tried to kill him. Doesn't that count for something? Maybe I'm reading into this too much, and he's just trying to gain my trust to make manipulating me that much easier.

Fuck. Why does his mind have to be so twisted? I hate not being able to read him while he seems able to read me like a damn book.

I keep my gaze focused on the gun in his hand. He promised me punishment for last night, and I can't help but wonder if this is it. A bullet straight through the head just like I had intended for him. At least it'll be quick that way. Though, if he's about to kill me, I'm not about to make it easier for him.

I cross my arms over my chest and send a scathing glare his way. "No," I demand, holding my ground.

Nic's head snaps up, his glare cutting through me like a warm knife through butter. His eyes bore into me, and I swallow back fear. That's not a stare I had ever hoped to have thrust upon me. It's scary as hell and has me almost desperate to wet my pants. He stalks toward me, and I find myself shrinking back into the bed. "Excuse me?" he questions as though just the idea of me being difficult is too much for his small mind to bear.

I stupidly raise my chin despite the way my hands shake. "You heard me."

With lightning-fast reflexes, Nic's hand shoots out. He grabs the front of my shirt and hauls me toward him, my feet scrambling beneath me as the bed disappears from under my body. He pulls me right in front of his hard body, his eyes mere inches from mine.

Nic hovers over me, a heavy scowl resting on his lips as his stare bores down on me. His chest rises and falls with rapid movements, and it's almost as though he needs a moment to gain control of himself.

He leans in, and I feel his breath brushing across the sensitive skin of my neck, his lips right beside my ear. "And you heard me," he murmurs in a deep, baritone voice that sends shivers careening over my skin. His hand falls to my waist and squeezes tight enough to leave a bruise, yet all I can focus on is his closeness and the way my body seems to heat under his stare. His other hand comes around to my lower back and drops down over my ass, squeezing it tight. "Now get this sweet as fuck ass out of my bunker and into the warehouse."

With that, he releases his hold on me and is gone in a flash, leaving me gasping for breath as he disappears through the small metal door.

I take a second to collect myself, but not risking a moment too long. I don't want to see what would happen if he had to come back for me. I play it smart and scramble after him, hoping to God that I'm not making a colossal mistake.

I hurry to the door, feeling as though I should be searching for that gun from last night, but I don't doubt that Nic has put that away somewhere only he can find. I doubt he's willing to risk something like that again.

I slip into my shoes—which have somehow made it to the top step—before grabbing the door handle and pausing. I take a shaky breath. Something tells me that whatever is about to happen on the other side of this door is going to mess with my head in the twisted, fucked-up way that only Nic knows how to do.

Finding the courage, I push open the door and slowly step out into the warehouse. The wide-open space is just as empty as I remember it from last night, only now, there's a body curled into the fetal position in the middle of the floor. Nic stands close by, leaning against a metal pillar, impatiently waiting.

His eyes are on mine, and they're heavy and intense but also filled with curiosity. Closing the door behind me, I face Nic front on and raise my chin before flicking my eyes down to the passed-out guy on the ground. "What is this?" I question, not wanting to get any closer.

Nic drops his gaze to a bucket that sits on the far wall. "Fill that with water," he orders before flicking his gaze to a sink in the opposite corner.

My gaze narrows. "Why?" I ask, hesitating as I glance at the bucket and then the unconscious man.

"He has to wake up somehow," Nic tells me, his voice calculating and terrifying. "It's your call, Roni. We can either sit and wait or we can get it over and done with."

I ball my hands into fists at my sides and clench my jaw, not liking this one bit, but I can't deny that sitting around and waiting to get this over and done with is going to kill me, so without waiting another second, I start for the bucket.

A short moment later, the water is nearly at the top, and I haul it out of the sink before hesitantly making my way towards Nic and the unconscious man. Water splashes on the ground as I walk, but I don't even notice it as Nic's eyes rest on mine.

I stop just short of them, not wanting to get much closer, but Nic indicates to the guy. "Pour it on him."

"No," I snap, glaring up at him and putting the bucket down at my feet. "I'm not about to be dragged into whatever bullshit games you're about to play here. Do your own dirty work."

Nic pushes off the metal pillar, and he seems to grow a million feet tall. "I said pour it on him," Nic growls in a chilling tone.

Letting out a defiant huff, I grab the stupid bucket and haul it at the dickhead on the ground, feeling sick with myself for how easily I caved. Why am I not stronger than this? I should be able to stand up to him, but the fear is too real.

The guy sucks in a deep gasp, his eyes springing open in shock. He instantly starts looking around, and the second he lays his eyes on Nic, he starts scrambling away from him. His eyes dart around the warehouse for some kind of exit, but Nic isn't that careless. If there were a way out of here right now, I'd already be running.

The guy can't keep his eyes off Nic, especially as he starts stalking him, moving forward like a python about to strike.

My chest rises and falls with rapid movements, watching the scene before me through wide, terrified eyes.

Nic draws a gun from behind his back, and I suck in a deep breath, but he doesn't take his eyes off the man, not even for a second. "Knees," he demands, the one word echoing through the empty warehouse like an ugly death sentence.

The guy blanches, and after quickly glancing at me, he realizes just how fucked he is. There's no getting out of here. This man will not live to see another day; it's just a fact.

He panics. "I … I … I …"

"KNEES. NOW," Nic booms, his tone making me flinch.

Tears fill the guy's eyes as he finally rises to his knees, his hands fall together in front of his chest, and he meets Nic's eyes. "Please, please. I swear, I'll hand myself in. I'll do anything you want. Please, I have a girl, a family. My mom … this will break her."

Nic steps into him, pressing his gun right against his temple as though he hadn't said a damn word. "You should have thought about that first," Nic rumbles, the words filling every inch of the warehouse.

"Yes, you're right. I should have thought of that first, but I've learned from my mistakes. I'll do anything. Please, just …"

A sick grin twists across Nic's face as he flinches the gun against the man's temple, moisture spreading down the front of his pants.

I stare in horror, unable to look away from the horrendous scene before me. "Nic," I seethe under my breath, desperation creeping through my veins. "Stop it. What are you doing? Who are you to decide if a man should live or die?"

Nic's eyes slice back to mine. "You're right," he says, his voice low and filled with a challenge. "I won't be deciding if he lives or dies. You will."

My mouth drops open. "What?" I breathe, instantly backing up a step, shaking my head viciously. He can't be serious. "No. I have nothing to do with this."

"Sure you do," Nic prompts, turning to face me and taking a step in my direction and then another. I back up a little more, glancing at the helpless man on the floor. Nic reaches out and grabs my wrist, hauling me into his chest and slamming the gun into my hand. "What's the matter, baby? You were so determined to kill a man last night. Now's your chance."

"No, I …" Fuck. This is that punishment he was talking about. He's going to force me to kill a man.

He walks away from me, and I instantly tighten my grip on the gun, the power rushing through my veins. He walks back toward the metal pillar, and the thought hits me that I could just shoot him in the back and end this once and for all. But my stomach clenches with the idea of killing a man like that.

Nic reaches his metal pillar and props himself against it like he had been earlier. "Well," he encourages. "What are you waiting for? Get it over and done with."

"No," I snap, instantly thinking of the girl and family the guy had mentioned earlier. I turn the gun on Nic, and just as I knew he would, he acts as though the gun doesn't even exist. "I'm not about to shoot him. I don't even know who he is or why he's here. I'm not an executioner, Nic. I don't have the right to decide who lives or dies, just like you don't. If he did something so awful, hand him over to the cops with a confession."

Nic laughs. "You have one bullet, Roni, don't waste it on me. Haven't you already learned that you don't have what it takes to kill me?"

"No," I say with a pissed off grunt. "We learned that your reflexes are faster than mine, that's all. I still pulled the trigger and had every intention of killing you."

Nic laughs and turns his gaze to the man on his knees. "Why don't you tell the pretty lady what it is that you did. Let her decide who should die today."

The guy swallows, his eyes going wide as he glances at me like a threat. But when he doesn't immediately start talking, Nic steps behind him and puts a knife to his throat … my fucking knife. "Talk," Nic demands, pulling tight on his hold and letting the blade pierce his skin just enough to send a trickle of blood trailing down his throat.

The guy meets my eyes again, and I watch with disgust as a grin starts pulling at his lips, making my stomach twist with nausea. Fondness and laughter shine through his eyes as if reliving the memories of whatever horrendous thing he did turns him on. "I killed them," he says, his voice low and menacing, a sound that will haunt me for the rest of my days. "I killed every last one of them but saved the little bitch for last, and while she screamed for help, begged for her dead mommy to come and rescue her, I fucked her, right in her bed with my hands around her throat, watching the life drain out of her."

I take a step closer, and not giving a shit that Nic stands right behind him, I pull the fucking trigger and send the bastard straight to hell.

CHAPTER 6

DOMINIC

Blood splatters over my face and shirt and I stare at the man in horror. I watch, almost in slow motion, as his body is rocked back from the force of the bullet, landing on the dirty ground with a heavy thump.

I scream, my eyes wide and filled with disgust as Nic takes a step back, blood soaking his clothes.

What did I just do?

My eyes drop to the dead man's face. I just killed him; I shot him and took his life.

I'm a murderer. Cold-blooded murderer.

I run.

I sprint toward the bunker, barging through the metal door as the sound of it rebounding off the wall echoes through my head like a sharp sting, or maybe I'm just hearing the gunshot on repeat.

I race through to the small bathroom and instantly meet my reflection in the shitty, cracked mirror above the sink. I look like a complete stranger. My eyes are wide, and the blood splattered over my face and clothes are a constant reminder of what I just did.

My hands curl around the fabric of my shirt, and I tear it over my head before viciously throwing it into the corner of the bathroom. I turn on the tap and instantly shove my hands under the stream of water, desperate to get rid of the blood. I pool water in my hands and lean over before splashing it over my face and scrubbing hard, unable to gain control of my rapid breathing.

What the hell have I just become? Maybe I'm more like my father and brother than I ever thought. Should I be crying? Why am I not crying? I should be disgusted with myself. I should be breaking down and hating what I did, but I can't.

I killed a man, and it felt amazing.

He deserved to die, and holding that gun gave me more power than any woman or man should ever be entitled to. Pulling that trigger and knowing I was the one responsible for sending his sick, twisted ass to the deepest pits of hell … fuck. The way he smirked and looked as though he was proud of what he did made me sick. Not to mention that the girl he was talking about … he didn't say her age, but it was clear that she was just a child.

Shit, I need to go back and make sure the fucker is dead. I need to shoot him again. I need a fucking ax and a crowbar. Only the sound of his bones crushing beneath my force will make me feel better now.

Nic was right all this time. I have darkness inside me, and now that I've let it out, I'm not sure I'll be able to reel it back in. I should be better—stronger. Fuck it, I don't even care if that gets me locked up for life. I will happily hand myself over.

Another gunshot rings out through the warehouse, and I jump at the sound, glancing back up in the mirror only to see the smeared blood over my face. I stare at myself. I should be ashamed, but I feel empowered. I feel alive. I feel ready to hail havoc down over anyone who has ever done me wrong.

I feel like a fucking queen.

My hands grip the side of the sink, squeezing tight while trying to force myself to remain still.

The bunker door flies open, and not a second later, Nic comes striding down the stairs. He stops in the kitchen, looking straight through to me in the bathroom, standing over the sink, and meeting my stare in the mirror.

He looks concerned, almost as though he's too scared to ask me how I feel. Maybe he didn't think I had the guts to pull the trigger. Maybe he thought I was a little bitch who would have shot him instead and fled.

He takes a step toward me, and I narrow my eyes, neither of us saying a word. He comes closer, and the tension rises between us. Blood stains his clothes worse than before, and I wonder if that second gunshot was him finishing the fucker off. Yet I can't seem to care—all that matters right now is Nic.

He reaches the entryway of the bathroom, and I straighten, still watching him through the mirror as he stops and rakes his eyes over my body. The intensity is too much. I hate him so bad for what he's made me do, and for what he's made me realize about myself. But the power still pulsing through my veins is too strong to worry about busting his ass over it just yet.

Nic clears his throat, getting ready to say something as he steps into the bathroom. His hands come to my waist, and he meets my eyes in the mirror again. Concern is etched over his features, and I don't doubt that he's about to hit me with the 'are you alright' bullshit, but that's the furthest from what I want.

He leans into me, and I feel his bloodied shirt pressing against my back. I should be disgusted … repulsed, yet a fire burns within me. I sense his questions about to come, but as his fingers tighten on my waist, I spin around and throw my arms around his neck, crushing a bruising kiss to his inviting lips.

Nic pauses for a second, probably wondering what the fuck is going on, but it takes no time at all for him to get on board with the plan.

I grab his shirt and tear it over his head, loving the feel of his warm skin against my body. A deep growl tears from within his chest, and he instantly takes control—but I don't give it willingly. My nails dig into his skin. I hate him so fucking much, but if he doesn't throw me against a wall and slam inside of me within the next two seconds, I really will kill the bastard.

Nic's tongue invades my mouth as his hands grip my body, tight enough to leave welcome bruises, and I feel myself pulling back. I tear my mouth from his, panting heavily, as I stare up at the man who has destroyed me time and time again.

Without warning, my hand slaps hard over his cheek, leaving a sharp sting in my palm. "I fucking hate you," I roar.

Nic stares at me, his eyes heating more and more by the second. He grabs my waist tighter and takes two forceful steps, slamming my body hard against the cold tiles of the bathroom wall. "I fucking hate you too," he tells me in the deep baritone voice that has me crushing my lips back to his and desperately reaching for his belt.

Nic reaches around me and unhooks my bra, and within seconds is tearing the fabric from my arms. The moment it's gone, his lips peel from mine, and I gasp for breath as his warm tongue runs down my neck, setting my body alight.

I get his pants undone and instantly slip my hand inside, not wasting time. My fingers curl around his hard, veiny cock, and my eyes close as the desperation tears through me. I work my hand all the way up and run my finger over his tip. If I wasn't so desperate to feel him inside, I'd be down on my knees, letting him fuck my mouth until tears welled in my eyes.

As my hand roams up and down his cock, his lips torture me, sucking and nipping at my skin, slowly working his way down to my tits. He sucks my nipple into his mouth, and as I squeeze his cock, he bites it, making me arch my back and press my chest into him.

His grip tightens on my waist, and within a second, he's shoving my pants to my ankles. I step free of them, and without warning, Nic grabs my ass and lifts me into his strong arms.

My arms fly around his neck to keep from falling as my legs spread wide, hooking around his waist. And then, in one quick thrust, Nic lines himself up with my pussy and buries himself deep inside, stretching me like never before. His head falls into the crook of my neck, and he groans low as I tip my head back to the wall and moan out his name.

My nails dig into his shoulders, and I feel the blood pooling beneath them. He instantly responds by biting down on mine, not hard enough to draw blood as he slowly pulls back out. He slams himself back in, and I cry out a gasp. "Fuck, yes," I call, needing so much more.

Nic doesn't disappoint and fucks me hard and fast against the bathroom wall, making me forget the world around me and the fucked-up situation he's put me in. All that matters is chasing that orgasm and finally feeling alive for the first time in years.

Our bodies grow sweaty and just when I think it's all about to be over, Nic peels me off the bathroom wall and walks me through to his bed. He throws me down, and my body crashes against the mattress. I want to scold him and remind him how much of an ass he is, but he flips me over, and I forget about everything but his hand spanking down across my ass. I welcome the sharp sting of his palm with a gasp before he slams right back inside of my soaking pussy with that large cock, stretching me until I'm seeing stars.

"Fuck," he growls, going so much deeper than he had been before, hitting that spot that drives me wild with need. "I missed this sweet pussy."

"Shut up and fuck me," I snap as my face squishes into the mattress. His fingers dig into my hips, and I can't help but reach through my legs to my aching clit and rub small, fast circles.

My eyes roll to the back of my head. I've never felt so fucking free, so wild, and powerful—I need it all. I need him to fuck me harder, give me everything he's got.

Nic's fingers come down to my pussy, playing in my wetness before I feel them at my ass. I instantly push back against them, and he gives me exactly what I want, pressing them into me and making me scream out. "Nic," I cry, rubbing harder at my clit as he fucks me like never before. "Harder. I need more."

He slams into me, completely giving himself to me as I push back against him, taking it all. My orgasm builds, and I clench my eyes, knowing it's going to tear through me like a fucking semitrailer.

His fingers push deeper in my ass, his cock harder in my pussy, and it hits me at all the right angles as though he knows my body better than I do. His hand slaps down over my ass, and I know it's going to leave a red mark. "Again," I pant.

Not one to disappoint, he gives it to me again and again until my orgasm tears through me, and my pussy clenches down around his hard cock, squeezing it with everything I've got. I feel Nic come hard inside of me, sending warm, fast spurts of cum shooting deep inside me as his fingers dig into my skin.

I've never felt anything quite so erotic, and I can't say that I've experienced angry, hate sex before, but if that's what it's like, I'll take it every fucking time. I'm used to guys going slow and steady, not willing to take any risks and truly read my body, but Nic … fuck.

He slowly pulls out of me, and as he does, I feel his heated stare on my body, watching as his cock slips out of my aching pussy along with his white beads of cum.

I don't dare move, loving how exposed I feel.

I feel his cum dripping down over my clit, and then his fingers are there, slowly rubbing it against me and instantly setting my body on fire. His slow, torturous circles drive me wild, and I clench my eyes, my body already so sensitive from the orgasm that pulsed through me.

I should be disgusted by him, pushing him away and telling him to fuck off, but I find myself here, wanting nothing more than to please him. I've never been so turned on. As he steps around the bed, keeping his fingers on my clit and his other hand slowly roaming up and down his cock, that's exactly what I do.

I open my mouth and lick up and down his massive length, tasting myself on his velvety skin. My tongue circles his tip, and as I look up at him, enclosing my mouth over his large cock, I notice the blood still covering his body, and it spurs me on. I suck his cock, keeping to the lazy rhythm of his fingers against my clit until he's coming down my throat and another orgasm is pulsing through me.

CHAPTER 7

DOMINIC

My fingers trail over her skin, brushing over her pebbled nipples and teasing her body as she lies in my arms. Her head resting against my chest is right where it's always belonged.

Roni's fingers play on my chest, and she traces the lines of my tattoos as we both try to catch our breaths. I hadn't expected that she'd come around to me quite so quickly, but the second her lips were on mine, I wasn't about to back down. Besides, I know every one of the fuckers who have kept her bed warm since we were last together, and I can guarantee this woman hasn't been thoroughly fucked in years. Who am I to say no?

She surprised the fuck out of me today. I knew she had it in her to pull that trigger, but I thought it was going to take a little more convincing than that. I was expecting a fight. I was expecting her to struggle with her inner demons, but the second the fucker explained what he'd done, she took justice into her own hands and proved once and for all just how fucking powerful she is.

She didn't hang around to show me just how much she enjoyed it, but I could tell by the look in her eyes that the adrenaline and power turned her on, just as it did for me.

She's always been so strong. She's always had the darkness in her soul, just like mine. We're kindred spirits, we always have been. She's just been too fucking stubborn to admit it. Roni has this need to be good, to do good, and to be the face of reason, but she's been lying to herself.

Welcome to the dark side, baby.

I can't say that I've ever fucked her like that before, but I loved it. It's as though her body was speaking to the darkest part of me, enticing me to give it everything I had. At that moment, I wanted to make her scream louder than she's ever screamed before. I wanted to feel her pussy pulsating and squeezing my cock. I wanted to give her everything.

She fucking deserved it.

Roni lets out a deep sigh, and I glance down at her beautiful face that hasn't changed a damn bit in twelve years. "What is it?" I question, not sure how things are going to be between us now. Does she still hate me, or is she all mine again? Maybe it's just angry, hate sex from here on out. If it is, that's honestly perfectly fine with me.

Roni pushes up off my chest and sits on the bed beside me, crossing her legs and looking down at my body, not ready to meet my eyes. "I don't know," she finally says. "I have too many things going through my head to even know where to begin with you."

"Start with the easiest," I say, realizing that this could go on for a while. Roni has always been the type to pick apart every little thing. She wants to know the reasons behind everything that happens, and then she'll go away and think about it some more.

"Okay," she says. "Well first, I need you to know that what you just made me do out there … that's not okay. I hate you for that. You forced me to give up a piece of me that I've been protecting, a piece that my father had always tried to take from me. I don't want to be like you. I'm not some psycho killer."

"But you enjoyed it," I tell her, pushing up onto my elbow and running my knuckles down the side of her face. "You liked the adrenaline, the power you felt holding that gun. You liked being the one who got to deliver justice and put the fucker down. You don't hate me, Roni. You hate that you're like me."

"I'm not," she rushes out. "I'm nothing like you."

"Just give it time, baby, and you'll see. You're just like me, but you have this wall up that you've buried it all behind. Don't you remember what it was like in high school? You used to love those parts of yourself, but then you went to college and learned how to hide it. This hoity-toity, stuck up chick that you're pretending to be, that's not the real Roni, and you know it. It's time to spread your wings."

Her eyes flick to mine for the briefest second, and the desire in her eyes tells me that she'd like nothing more than to slip back into the girl she used to be and truly let her shine. But in a second, she glances away, and that look in her eyes vanishes. "You're insane," she tells me. "That was just high school bullshit trying to look tough in front of my boyfriend. That wasn't who I was. This here, the woman who sits before you, this is the real me, and you need to stop trying to make me into someone I'm not. She doesn't exist anymore."

I reach out and rest my hand on her knee. "I hate to break it to you, baby, but that girl still exists. You've just hidden her away and now she's dying to break free."

Roni rolls her eyes and looks back toward the kitchen, not wanting to face me at all. "You've killed every boyfriend I've had over the past twelve years. At a certain point—I just stopped trying."

I scoff. "Come on," I laugh. "Give me credit. I only killed one of them because he was an ass and doing you wrong. The rest were pussy enough to run at the first sign of a threat. If they had the balls to stand up to me, sure, maybe I would have let them hang around a little while longer."

Her eyes flash to mine. "What are you talking about? Every single one of them disappeared, and I never heard from them again—not even their families heard from them. Don't lie to me. You killed them."

"I swear," I tell her. "Seven years ago. I slaughtered one like the fucking pig that he was. Wearing my fucking mark while fucking my girl and doing her wrong. I wasn't going to stand by that shit."

"What are you talking about?" Roni demands. "I never dated any

Widows."

"Yeah, baby," I laugh. "You sure fucking did. Edmond Travers. Once I found you in Bellevue Springs, I put him in your life to keep an eye on you. Only he snuck his way into your bed and your heart and then fucked every hooker that came through my clubhouse. I wasn't going to stand for it, so I waited until he fucked-up one of my deals and ended him. I didn't realize that you'd fallen for him. If I knew, I would have only fucked him up a bit."

Roni sucks in a gasp, her eyes finally coming back to mine, but she slowly starts shaking her head. "I … I wasn't in love with him. With any of them, actually."

I narrow my eyes at her. "Then what's the problem?"

"I just … you can't just go around killing whoever you want."

"And why not?" I question, pulling her down and rolling on top of her, bracing myself with my elbow to not squish her. I dip my head into her neck. "You just did and don't try to deny how good it felt," I say, grinding down against her and loving the way she squirms beneath me. "You fucking loved it. It made you feel alive. I saw it in your eyes. You, baby girl, are just like me. Right down to the bone."

Roni presses her hands against my chest and forces me back, putting a bit of space between us. "You're an asshole."

"Never claimed that I wasn't."

She keeps pushing until I'm completely off her, and she slips off my bed. "I have to get some air."

I nod, watching as she gets up from the bed and takes two steps toward my dresser. She opens the top drawer and pulls one of my shirts over her head. It falls right to her knees, and I struggle with the devastation of not being able to see her body opposed to the joy that rushes through me at seeing her in my clothes.

She makes her way to the door, only glancing back at me once, but the look in her eyes speaks volumes.

I stay where I am as she walks out of the bunker. If she were running, she'd have worn something else and gone for her shoes or the car keys, but as it is, I feel that I can trust her and some part of me is screaming that she doesn't want to leave. She wants to stay right here and see where this roller coaster is going to lead.

Ten minutes turn to twenty, and when the thirty-minute mark starts approaching and she's not back, I climb out of bed and go after her. It's nearing the middle of the afternoon, and I don't doubt that she's hungry. The Roni I knew back in high school could eat a fucking horse and still have room for dessert, not to mention the way she used to throw back coffee. She's got to be dying for one of those.

I make my way out of the bunker, and the first thing I notice is the empty space on the floor and the lack of blood spread out over the concrete. The boys must have come to get rid of that dickhead's body. Usually, they would have stopped by to let me know, but judging from the timeframe, I would have been balls deep with Roni screaming my name while they were here. Maybe it's a good thing they didn't stop to chat.

I glance around the warehouse and raise my brow as I look out the back entrance to where sunlight is streaming in, and the big roller door is wide open for the world to see.

That roller door had an industrial-sized padlock and a chain keeping it locked, and somehow, Roni has broken through it. She sits out on the grassy area behind the warehouse, and I watch her with a raised brow. The door was open, she could have run and gone back home, though I would have found her stubborn ass and brought her right back, but she didn't. She sat out in the sun and stayed.

I watch her for a few moments, sitting back in the grass with her head tipped back, raised to the sun and soaking up the rays. She's fucking beautiful. Her blonde hair reflects the sun and makes it look almost as though she wears a halo, which is ironic when you consider that she shot a man today. She didn't kill him, though. Her shot went straight through his shoulder, and while she sent him sprawling out on the ground and bleeding, it wasn't a kill shot. That came later.

She turns to look at me as she hears me striding toward her. "Hungry?" I ask, looking down at her sun-kissed cheeks.

Her eyes rake over my body, and as her stare begins to heat, she slowly spreads her legs, revealing everything that's hidden beneath my shirt. "Starving."

Fuck me.

My dick hardens, and I try and figure out the quickest way to get her back to my bed. Fuck eating—I can shove food down her throat later. "Let's go then."

Roni shakes her head and I watch as defiance shines brightly through her eyes. "No," she tells me. "If we're doing this, then I'm taking control." She pats the grass beside her. "Sit your ass down, Nic. It's my turn to fuck you, and I'm going to do it right here for the world to see."

CHAPTER 8

RONI

My feet rest upon the table as I study the knife in my hands. It's been just over a week, and I don't think I've ever fucked so much in my life. My pussy is always throbbing and aching but in the best kind of way.

Nic has held me here, not allowing me to leave the warehouse but he's certainly given me my freedom. It's like I'm playing the role of his girlfriend again, and we're locked away on vacation. Only instead of a tropical beach, it's a dirty as fuck bunker hidden beneath a warehouse.

I've gotten to know the real Nic, and while he's exactly as I always remembered, I'm quickly realizing that I don't hate him like I've always told myself. He's a monster, but he always has a method to his madness.

Over the past week, I've watched him kill three men, and each of them have deserved it more than the last. As soon as he's done, a fire lights in his eyes, and he fucks me until I'm screaming his name—sometimes still with his victim's blood all over his body. For some reason, knowing he holds that kind of power gets me hotter than I've ever been before.

Nic was right. I fucking love it. I have darkness inside me, and the more I encourage that part of me to shine, the less I'm starting to hate my time here. I miss my life and hate that I'm away from my patients, but when I think about it, I probably need a therapist more than they do.

I haven't shot anyone since the guy at the beginning, but the more and more that I watch Nic, the more I feel that I could. It's a dangerous game he has me playing, one that could destroy me.

Am I sick? Maybe I'm just twisted like Nic, but either way, I don't want to go home.

Nic steps out of the bathroom, a towel around his waist as his strong muscles roll with his movement. He stops by his dresser. "Get dressed," he tells me. "The cops have stopped searching around here. We can go and pick up something to eat, but then I have a job."

"Oh?" I ask, getting up from the table and leaving the knife behind. I bite down on my lip, not sure how far I could push this. "What kind of job? Can I come?"

Nic stops what he's doing and looks over at me as I make my way toward him. "I need to address the Widows, let them know what's going on. I don't think it's a good idea for you to be there."

"You think I can't handle it?"

"I think they can't handle it," he says, leaning into me. He brushes his knuckles down my cheek before grabbing my chin and forcing my stare back to his. "We'll get dinner and then I'll drop you back here. I'll only be gone an hour. I wanna get back here so I can run my tongue through your sweet cunt."

Need washes through me. "Why wait?" I ask, feeling my pussy pulsing with anticipation.

Nic looks down at me, torn by the invitation and the need to get out of here to get to his Widow's meeting on time, but when he drops his towel to reveal his stiff cock begging for my attention, I know I've got him exactly where I need him.

Nic grabs me with lightning-fast reflexes and throws me up into the air. His arms hook under my legs and I have to grab hold of his head just to keep from falling on the ground. He perches me on top of his tall dresser and instantly spreads my legs as wide as they can go, revealing my already naked self to him.

I've been living in nothing but his shirts over the past week and the choice to not wear any panties has definitely worked in my favor multiple times.

Nic meets my eyes, and as his tongue runs over his bottom lip, I know I'm in for a good ride. My pussy is nearly at his head height, and as it throbs for him, his eyes grow excited with need.

I watch as he takes hold of his cock and starts working his hand up and down it, not one to miss out on pleasure where it's being given. "You ready, babe?" he questions. "This is gonna be fast."

His head finally dips between my legs and being a man of his word, I instantly feel his tongue swiping through my pussy and putting me out of my misery.

Thirty minutes later, I sit in his shitty little car, wearing pants for the first time all week. He speeds through the streets of Breakers Flats as though he knows them better than the back of his hands. "Are you sure this is a good idea?" I ask, nervously glancing around and making sure no one stares at Nic's car for longer than necessary. Though no one around here would be stupid enough to rat Nic out to the cops— that's just asking for a death sentence.

"It's fine," he says. "I've already called in the order. You can go in and get it. I don't even need to get out of the car. No one is going to see me."

"This is just asking for trouble."

Nic glances across at me, his eyes shining with excitement. "I know."

"You're such an idiot," I laugh as he pulls up outside a restaurant. Nic glances at me again and I narrow my eyes in suspicion. "Is this some kind of test to make sure I don't run away? Do you know how easy it would be to slip into the crowd and leave?"

Nic gives me a cocky grin and winks. "You won't leave."

I raise a brow. "How do you know that? I hope you're not expecting me to get some form of Stockholm syndrome and fall madly in love with you."

"Here's to hoping," he says, the corner of his mouth pulling up into a confident smirk. "Besides, judging by the way you're constantly riding my dick, I'd say you're already there."

"Being in love with your cock is very different from being in love with you. Trust me," I say, swinging open the door and grabbing the cash in the center console. "I'm just using you for good sex. I still think you're an asshole."

I get out and slam the door before he gets a chance to say anything back and hurry inside. Despite how easy it would be to make a run for it, I'm kinda hungry, and the thought of actually walking away from Nic right now doesn't sit well with me.

I have to make this fast. Nic could be caught by anyone out there, and although he belongs in prison, I'm not quite done having my fun with him yet. Maybe he's onto something about being in love with him. I mean ... I'm definitely not, but I'm certainly feeling all those good things I felt back in high school. The rush when he's around, the butterflies when he walks into a room, the need to always be close to him—shit. Maybe I am starting to feel something for him again. If that's the case, I definitely need therapy. There's gotta be something wrong with me. Who falls in love with a murderer?

Another murderer, that's who.

I get our dinner and hurry back out to his car, knowing that we have to get back to the warehouse and eat before he runs off again to remind his fellow douchebags that he's the king of all the douchebags.

My thought has a cheesy smirk ripping across my face, and as I drop down into Nic's probably stolen car, he glances at me with a curious stare. "What?" he grunts, refusing to take his eyes off me until I answer.

"Nothing," I say with a laugh. "Just drive before I'm reminded how awful you look in orange."

Nic rolls his eyes but steps on the gas and sends us soaring down the road. We get all of a hundred meters before Nic is grabbing the food off my lap and picking at all his favorites. "Hey," I snap, slapping his hand away. "Get your filthy hands out of there. Is it really that hard to wait until we get back?"

"Can't," he grunts. "Ran out of time eating your pussy. Eat up, we're going straight to the Widows."

My eyes widen and excitement settles through me. The second he mentioned going out to see them, I was curious to see him in action, and not just the action of getting his dick wet or ending a life, but seeing him truly as the leader of the Black Widows. I want to see how they respect him, I want to see how they act around him, how they jump at his commands.

I want to see my man dominate.

My man? Fuck. No, I can't start thinking like that. I know it feels like he's always been mine, even when he wasn't, but that can't be the case. I have to get a little separation between us before I completely get pulled into his trap. I wonder what he'll do if I tuck and roll right out of the car onto the highway.

Nic has a reputation around here and that reputation has spread far and wide. It'll be interesting to see if his men still fear him after six and a half years away or if they're going to need a reminder of why he's the best in the business.

Knowing that we won't be stopping to eat, I start pulling out our dinner and hand Nic his burger and fries to avoid him constantly reaching over and bugging the living shit out of me. Nic drives effortlessly while practically annihilating his food and I get halfway through before turning to him. "Will you tell me what it was like in prison?"

His brows crease and he looks over at me while popping a chip into his mouth. "Why do you wanna know that?"

I shrug my shoulders. "Just curious," I say with a grin pulling at my lips. "Best to know what it's like seeing as though I'll be heading that way if I spend much more time with you."

Nic rolls his eyes and focuses back on the road. "The first year was the worst. Adjusting and figuring out the hierarchy in there while also trying to show those other dickheads that I couldn't be fucked with wasn't exactly fun. It was rough, but they quickly learned who I was and that if they tried, they'd end up in the morgue. I sent three fuckers to their graves in the first two months. I couldn't confirm it, but I'm pretty sure there were some Wolves in there or at least some guys with connections to the Wolves."

"You're Dominic Garcia," I remind him. "You were just starting in prison right when the Wolves were screwing around with their leadership. Everyone would have tried to take you out just to claim they deserved the top spot."

Nic nods. "And that's exactly what happened. No one could even get close and the ones who tried ended up dead. People on the inside weren't the only ones learning those lessons the hard way."

"Well, shit," I grumble, unable to even begin imagining what that would have been like "What happened after that?"

"When the death threats slowed down a little, I was able to start focusing on making connections and learning how to screw the system. After I got a few guards in my back pocket, life was pretty smooth. I ran that prison like I run my Widows."

"Is that how you were able to break out of there so easily?"

Nic scoffs. "There was nothing easy about it, but yes, having the guards under my thumb certainly helped."

I shake my head. "I can't even—"

Nic's phone blares through the car, cutting off our conversation. He glances down at the screen and groans before hitting accept and lifting the phone to his ear. "Kai?" he snaps, sounding pissed to have our conversation interrupted.

There's a short silence, and I try to listen to Kairo's voice coming through the phone, but his words are too rushed and muffled to understand what the fuck is going on.

"FUCK," Nic roars, quickly glancing at me before stepping on the gas and pushing his car to its limits. "I'll be there in two fucking minutes."

Nic ends the call and practically throws the phone down on the ground so he can use both hands to drive. "What's going on?" I ask, wide-eyed, feeling panic settle through me at the tense set of his brows.

Nic's lips pulls into a tight line, and for a moment, I wonder if he's not going to answer me before he finally starts talking. "Christian got wind of me coming here tonight. So not only is one of my men a fucking traitor, but the Wolves are on their way."

"WHAT?" I screech. "But they'll kill you. Christian won't stop until you're dead. You have to go. I know my brother, and when he's trying to prove a point, he's ruthless."

Nic shakes his head, looking disgusted at my suggestion. "I'm not about to abandon my men and serve them up on a silver platter for your brother to take out. If there's a threat, you bet your fucking ass that I'll be standing there front and center."

"But …" I cut myself off, not really knowing what to say but not doubting that a face-off tonight will mean war. It'll be a massacre, just like the one nearly seven years ago. Both Christian and Nic got lucky that night, but their luck is bound to run out at some point, and if either one of them died tonight, I don't think I could survive.

Christian is my big brother, he's my flesh and blood. I love him with everything that I have, but Nic … fuck. I don't even know what he is to me right now, but the thought of him bleeding out on the ground of some dirty warehouse makes me sick. This can't happen. One of them has to back down, but they're both far too stubborn to be the one to bend.

I guess the only question is; when it comes down to it, when the war breaks out right before my eyes, what side am I fighting for?

Nausea pulses through me and I try to keep my dinner down as Nic speeds through the streets. He reaches the Widows clubhouse in record time and just as his car pulls into the drive, the roller door is instantly lifted to find the whole place a flurry of activity.

Tattooed men race around the clubhouse, each armed and dangerous. Three guys hurry toward Nic's car and I instantly recognize

Kairo, Sebastian, and Elijah. Nic gets out of the car, and when their eyes fall to me, they come to a screeching halt.

I get out of the car and as I make my way around to Nic, someone else jumps straight into his vacated driver's seat and takes his car away like some kind of valet service. "What the fuck is she still doing here?" Kairo demands, seething at Nic as his eyes flick back to me. "She was supposed to be gone."

"Chill out," Nic snaps. "She's fucking bait. Just wait until Christian sees her. It'll be fucking over for him."

My back straightens, and as Kairo and Sebastian look back at me again, Nic follows their stares as if only just realizing that I'm close enough to have heard every word.

Nic turns on me, his eyes wide and frantic, knowing that a threat is coming and that he doesn't have a chance in hell of dealing with me before having to get himself ready. "Fuck you," I snap, the sting of his words piercing my chest like a steel rod right through the heart. My hand snaps out and the blow across his face is loud enough to echo through the whole warehouse like a gunshot.

I should have run when I had the chance. What was I thinking sticking around and letting him play me like that? I was supposed to be smarter.

Tears fill my eyes and instead of sticking around and playing some twisted role in his little gang war, I turn and run for the door, knowing I only have a matter of seconds to get out of here before ending up right in the crosshairs of a shootout.

I hear Nic come for me and as my name roars on his lips, I glance back just in time to see Elijah catch his elbow and pull him back. "Let her go," Elijah says, waving me off as though I'm nothing. "We have bigger things to deal with."

I don't wait around to hear anymore, just keep running full force ahead, straight for the door, knowing that not tonight, but soon enough, he will come for me again, but this time, it's going to be different.

I finally reach the door and haul it open before breaking out into the night but as I run down the long drive of the Widows clubhouse, at least thirty cars come screeching to a stop before me, blocking me in with their headlights all aimed at me.

Nowhere to run. Nowhere to hide.

Then in the blink of an eye, hundreds of Wolves stand before me each with a gun aimed right at my chest.

CHAPTER 9

DOMINIC

Gunshots echo through the clubhouse, and I instantly get flashbacks from seven years ago when I stood in this very spot and defended my men. I did it then, and I'm doing it now. The only difference is, back then, Roni wasn't running around my fucking clubhouse with some kind of need to prove herself.

I hate that she overheard that bullshit. I didn't mean a fucking word of it, but I wasn't ready to explain to the boys what the fuck is going on. It was the easy option and I fucking took it. I know the past week with her hasn't exactly gone down the way a usual relationship would, but I fucking loved it. It's been the best week, despite the few hurdles we had to climb over at the beginning.

I fucked it all up, and now she's out there, running around with a bunch of Wolves, but being Mikhail Russo's long-lost daughter, at least she'll be safe with them. I hope. Christian would lay down his life before letting harm come her way, but she's been gone a long time, and running out of my clubhouse, she could have easily been mistaken for one of our girls.

If anything fucking happens to her, I won't stop until I've wiped those fucking Wolves out of existence.

More gunfire sounds through the clubhouse and all my boys fall in line, exactly how they've trained, ready to defend their leader, their brotherhood, and their home. My snipers sit up on the roof, ready to defend us, and as more gunfire sounds, I realize that they're trying to break through our locks.

Bullets shoot through my roller doors and everyone ducks, knowing just how lethal a blind bullet can be, but it's only another second before the roller door shoots up and over a hundred Wolves are bearing down on my men.

We match them equally with numbers, if not more, making me thankful that we had decided to have a meeting tonight. Otherwise, only a handful of men would have been here waiting and would have been slaughtered like cattle.

My Widows charge, meeting them face to face.

Gunshots sound through my clubhouse, and with each one, my anger only burns stronger. No one comes in here and disrespects my home like this. They will not get away with this. I will slaughter every single one of them … I just have to know that Roni is safe first.

I push forward into the crowd of Wolves, knowing that each of them sees me with a target on my back, but I won't be stopping. I will not go down until I know where she is. I hold my gun tight in one hand while my knife rests comfortably in my other, just as my father always taught me.

Most of the gun power is starting to ease as everyone flies through their ammo, having to use their fists, which honestly, I prefer. My guys are good, but they're nothing against a gun. With a fistfight, though, my guys will dominate. Every. Fucking. Time.

I try to ignore the fallen bodies around me, some mine, some Wolves. I can concentrate on that shit afterward. For now, I have a job to do.

Dumb fuckers come at me left, right, and center, every single one of them wanting a piece of the guy who burned down their home seven years ago. I spot my boys Kairo, Elijah, and Sebastian and see that each of them is still doing fine, which sends relief shooting through me with a new energy to keep going. My boys are my brothers, and without them, I have nothing.

The men coming for me drop like flies. They're no match for me. The only one who could even come close to giving me a fair fight is Christian, and so far, the fucker is nowhere to be seen, but I know he's here. There's no way he would miss all the fun.

I hear a loud squeal that speaks right to my soul. It's the same squeal I heard when I forced myself into her apartment, the same one that comes tearing through the small bunker every time I throw her down on my bed, the same one I would die for.

I start searching frantically, my distraction allowing the Wolves to land more than their fair share of punches. A blade comes flying past my face and slicing through the side of my cheek. I have to put Roni to the back of my mind, even if only for a second.

I grab the bastard with the knife and snap his wrist in one quick blow before bending his fucking arm back and stabbing the dickhead right in the gut, watching as he drops to the ground.

I send a quick, unexpected blow to the fucker next in line, instantly knocking him out before scanning the room in a panic. Where is she? Come on, Roni, speak to me. Tell me where the fuck you are.

As if on cue, I hear a soft groan followed by her defiant, "Don't ever fucking touch me again, prick," and I whip my head around, seeking her out.

Her eyes are wide and haunted, and I glance over her shoulder to figure out if the guy she just brought to his knees was one of mine or Christian's. If he's Christian's, he's going to die anyway, but if he's one of mine, he's going to face the firing squad if I find that he put his hands on my girl.

Roni catches my panicked gaze, and within a heartbeat, she starts racing toward me, the words I'd said long forgotten. "RONI," I yell, breaking away from the guy who tries to stab me in the back.

She keeps her wide stare locked on mine as she runs, weaving through the men and terrified for her life. A gunshot rings out behind her and she instantly drops to the ground with a loud squeal. She's strong, and while she's just starting to open herself to the darkness, a gang war isn't exactly something that she was ready for.

I reach her in no time, scooping her right off the ground and placing her on her feet. I curl my hand around her arm tight enough to leave bruises and run, desperate to get her out of here.

"Are you hurt?" I yell back over my shoulder, taking in her panicked face as we race through the clubhouse.

She shakes her head, too crazed to even respond.

I squeeze her arm, trying to get her to focus. "Where's your brother?"

Roni blinks a few times and takes a shaky breath before finally wrapping her head around all the bullshit and answering. "I don't know. I saw him outside and haven't seen him since. Why? You're not going to hurt him."

"I'll do more than fucking hurt him after he brought this bullshit down on my men."

Roni cringes, and for a moment I hate myself for being so ruthless and open about my plans for her big brother, but fuck it, I won't be hiding it. Surely she knows that he signed his own damn death certificate by coming here like this tonight.

She doesn't comment on her brother's impending doom, and I take it for what it is—an argument not worth having right now.

When she trips over a discarded body, I tighten my grip on her and keep her moving. I won't be letting her fall behind. She will not get hurt under my watch.

We're just about to the back offices where I can lock her away from threats when five men come at me from all sides. Roni tugs on my hand, forcing me to a stop knowing that if I keep going, we're both going to end up dead. They bear down on us and I instantly push her behind me. "Don't fucking move," I tell her, ready to protect her with my fucking life if that's what it takes.

The Wolves come at me, and I do everything that I can to keep myself in front of her, but with five guys all looking for a piece of me, it's not always that easy. Not to mention, now the Wolves see her as somebody I want to protect. The target on her back may even be bigger than mine.

Fists come at my face while a knife slices straight through my fucking waist, missing anything important, but stinging enough to make me realize that I'm not going to get out of this alive.

Roni screams behind me, absolutely terrified, but I'll be damned if I ever give her up. Another gunshot rings out and as my energy starts draining out of me, more punches start getting through. I can't hold them off, I'm going to fucking lose her.

As if sensing that I'm in trouble, Kairo, Elijah, and Sebastian show up at my side and their presence has a newfound energy powering through me.

Kairo moves in beside me, grunting as he delivers a crowd-pleasing blow to the fucker attempting to take his life. "What are you doing?" he growls through a clenched jaw. "Hand her over and this will all be over. You're going to get yourself killed."

I send a sharp glare his way while narrowly avoiding another bullet that shoots right past my face. Realizing this isn't the time to fuck around, I come clean, finally letting them know what's up. "I'll fucking die before giving her up," I spit. "I've been in love with her since I was sixteen."

I hear Roni's gasp behind me as Kai's eyes bug out of his head, but in an instant, he's with me just like I knew he would be, ready to protect her with everything that he has. If she's worthy of capturing me like that, then my boys will protect her with their lives despite her blood. It's just the way things are around here.

More and more men come at us, and the fight quickly moves to the back of my clubhouse, everyone following us to either protect or attack. Fists fly back and forth, while guns, knives, and brass knuckles get more action than they've ever seen before.

As another Wolf falls to the ground, I glance back at Roni, making sure that she's alright, only to find her gone. Panic surges through me, but as I begin scanning the room, I find her standing on the other side of Sebastian with her battle face on and a crowbar securely in her hand, going to fucking town.

I can't help but grin.

That's my fucking girl, and damn, it's the sexiest thing I've ever seen.

Sebastian stands right by her, letting her do her thing while always keeping her in his sights, allowing me the freedom to fight like I should be fighting.

The war rages on, and men drop around me, learning once and for all that Dominic Garcia and the Black Widows can't be fucked with.

Blood seeps from my stab wound but I keep fighting. Bodies fly across the warehouse like fucking bowling balls, while the random gunshots continue to send shivers down my spine, not knowing if it's one of my men or the enemy.

As men surround me, breaking bottles over heads, wielding knives that drip with their enemy's blood, the lines seem to blur between my side and theirs.

A familiar face finally makes its way to me, and I stare at Christian with disgust. How could he bring his men into this? I once thought he was a good guy, but it seems that he's more like his father than anyone ever expected. The seven years of leading the Wolves has changed him.

"WHERE IS SHE?" he bellows, cutting straight to the chase and drawing his gun, pointing it right between my eyes.

I smile, shaking my head before spitting a mouthful of blood to the ground. I step into his gun, letting the cold metal press right against my forehead. I stare into his eyes, leader against leader, and tell him exactly how it is. "You better pull the fucking trigger because you'll never get her."

Darkness swirls in Christian's eyes, and I know without a doubt that he won't hesitate, but when I hear Roni's scream tearing through the clubhouse, we both whip our gazes toward her.

She runs at us. "NOOOOO," she screams, reaching her brother in seconds and knocking his arm out of the way. "Don't fucking touch him," she demands, throwing herself in front of me and refusing to move as she stares down her older brother. "Take your fucking Wolves and leave."

He gapes in horror, unable to believe what the fuck he's seeing, but he's not having it. I go to grab her, hooking my arm around her waist and getting ready to haul her stubborn ass behind me, but Christian launches out and grips her by the arm, desperately trying to tear her away.

Roni gets stuck in a twisted tug of war and screams in pain as he yanks on her arm. "Don't be a fucking idiot," he seethes at his little sister before shooting a wicked glare my way. "Let go of her, or I swear I will fucking end you all."

Roni tries to push at Christian's chest, kicking her legs and trying to get free. "Let me go. I'm not going with you."

Christian shakes his head, having enough of this ridiculous little game. His gun comes up, and without even thinking about it, he pulls the trigger, narrowly missing Roni's face before the bullet sinks deep into my chest.

I'm rocked back with the force, my body slamming heavily to the hard ground while Roni's screams are the last thing I hear before everything goes quiet.

CHAPTER 10

RONI

"YOU'RE FUCKING DOMINIC GARCIA?" Christian roars as his office door slams shut behind him, blocking out the sound of the Wolves desperately trying to keep one another alive.

I fly to my feet after being thrown across his office into the shitty little couch in the corner of the room. "I'm not some fucking animal that you get to boss around and manhandle," I scream, storming across the office and getting right in his face. "I can fuck whoever the hell I want to fuck. It's none of your damn business. I'm twenty-eight years old, not some hopeless teenage girl who doesn't know what the fuck she's doing. Now get out of my way. I have to go and check that he's still fucking breathing."

Christian grabs my arm and pushes me back toward the couch. "Like hell. Are you in-fucking-sane? The dickhead just broke out of prison. Prison, Roni. He's a fucking criminal. You're so much better than that. I didn't risk everything for you to fall back into this fucked-up trap. You were supposed to be a fucking star. You were supposed to have it all, but you're throwing it away for a quick fuck with a guy who's either going to be dead in a few years or locked back up. You have too much to live for, and I'm not about to let you waste it on him."

I storm back toward him. "Manhandle me one more fucking time, Christian, and I swear to God, I will fuck things up for you so bad …"

"Oh yeah," he scoffs. "How the fuck do you think you're going to do that? I'm your brother. I have every right to manhandle you if I think you're making the biggest fucking mistake of your life."

I slam my hands against his chest. "Brother?" I shriek. "Brother. So, now all of a sudden, you want to be my brother. Guess what, dickhead? You haven't been my brother for years. A brother is supposed to be there for his sister, not some distant memory. You've lost whatever right you think you had. You're nothing but a stranger to me now. Look at you," I scoff, running my eyes up and down his lean body, taking in the battle wounds covering him from head to toe. "You're not the brother I once knew."

Christian grabs me and pulls me into him, scowling down at me. "You don't get to talk to me like that."

"News flash, big brother," I say, the distaste thick in my tone, wishing this was already over and done with so I can make sure that

Nic is still alive. "I don't bow down to you. I'm not one of your loyal followers. I can talk to you however the hell I want, and seeing as you're solely responsible for the deaths of at least thirty people tonight, I'll promise to never speak a fucking word to you ever again. I hate you for what you did. How could you do that? They were people just like you and me. They had jobs, lives, families, children. You're a monster, just like Dad was."

Christian releases his grip on me, anger bubbling out of him in waves. "I'm nothing like him," he seethes. "And for the record, the road goes both ways. I've done nothing but look out for you from afar. I've made sure you were safe. I made sure you always got whatever the fuck you wanted. Is that something your father would have done? Fuck no. I'm nothing like him, so you better watch your fucking mouth before you go and accuse me of that bullshit. You, on the other hand, when was the last time you tried reaching out to me? I don't see you blowing up my phone every day and checking in. You're just as much of a shitty sister as I am of a brother."

I narrow my gaze at him, knowing he's damn right, but I'm far too stubborn and pissed off to actually acknowledge it. He doesn't deserve that.

"You killed countless men tonight."

"What did you think I was going to do? Dominic Garcia kidnapped you right from your apartment. Do you really think I was about to sit back and let him keep hurting you like that? Fuck that, I have more than enough men in there to know what was going on. Though, it turns out that I had nothing to worry about. You were too fucking busy fucking the guy to remember that he kidnapped you from your home."

I shake my head. "No, that's not what this was about. No one even knew I was gone."

"Are you fucking kidding me? You're my sister. I knew the fucking second you were gone. With Dominic's face all over the news, and his last known location heading toward Bellevue Springs, I knew he was coming for you. It was only a matter of finding you."

"No, don't put this on my shoulders," I snap. "You did this as a power play. You wanted to be the one to kill Nic and take the glory, just like Dad wanted seven years ago."

Christian walks around to the desk and drops down into his seat. "I told you, Roni," he says, slowly glancing back up at me. "I'm nothing like Dad. This had nothing to do with making a power play. Look around you; I already have the fucking power. Believe it or not, this was all about rescuing my baby sister. I know you don't think so, but I fucking love you. You're the only real family I have left, and you bet your ass that I'd start a whole fucking gang war just to make sure you were safe. There's nothing I wouldn't do for you, kid."

My gaze drops to the dirty floor. "I'm not a kid anymore."

"Yeah," he scoffs. "I'm starting to realize that."

My eyes sweep back up to his and I bite the inside of my cheek, hating that I have to say what I'm about to say. Regret courses through me, and I swallow down fear as his stare bores into mine. "I didn't need to be rescued, Christian. I was happy."

"Happy?" he scoffs. "No, I don't believe that for one second.

You've been running from the guy since you were sixteen."

"I know, I just … it's different now. I think I'm in lo—"

Christian flies to his feet, his finger pointed right at me, his face turning a deep shade of red. "DON'T YOU DARE SAY THAT YOU'RE IN LOVE WITH HIM," Christian roars, cutting me off. "That's unacceptable. I will not stand for this."

"I don't give a shit what you stand for. I can't help the way I feel."

"He's no good for you."

I scoff. "He's everything. He may not be able to show his face in public and we will never be able to have a normal relationship, but that doesn't change the fact that every time he's around me, everything seems right in the world."

Christian shakes his head, almost as though he can't even comprehend what I'm saying. "Dominic Garcia is incapable of loving anyone except himself. He'll screw you over and leave you for dead. I forbid it. You're not to see him."

"Seriously, Christian," I say, reminding him just how stubborn I can be. "The more you try to deny me, the harder I'm going to try to go back to him. Besides, I'm an adult, and I don't need your approval for anything I do."

He shakes his head. "You're an idiot. Nothing good will come from this."

"You're wrong about him. He's not the guy you think he is."

"Bullshit," he laughs. "You've spent a week with him. I've spent years figuring out who he really is. He's not the guy for you. Go back to Bellevue Springs, pack up your life, and move somewhere else where he can't find you. Then find some dipshit accountant who will make you happy and stay away from the Widows. That's the end of this conversation. I never wanna hear about it again."

I get up and walk to the door before stopping and looking back at the brother I once loved with my whole heart. "He protected me in that clubhouse. He would have laid his life down just so I wouldn't get hurt, and I know you saw it. He's not a bad guy; he just does bullshit things like you do because that's what his position demands of him. You can't act like you don't understand that. Now, I know he killed Dad seven years ago, and he's done some really fucked-up things, but whether or not you like it, I'm going to be with him."

I grab the door handle and pull it open, but Christian's bitter scoff stops me in my tracks. "He doesn't get to take the credit for bringing down the leader of the fucking West Side Wolves. He fucking wishes he could have put the bullet between Dad's eyes."

"What?" I grunt. "No. It was all over the news. The Widows claimed that kill was theirs, and we all know that Nic would have been the one to do it."

"No," Christian snaps. "It was Snake. One of Dad's own men betrayed him during the fire and shot him right through the eyes. Your precious Widows had nothing to do with it."

My brows raise as my mouth drops open. All these years, I assumed Nic was the one to pull the trigger, and while I was thankful to have my father gone for good, I couldn't find it within me to be angry at him. I was more cut up about him ending Edmond after we dated for less than three months, but it turns out I should have been thankful for that one too.

I nod my head and go to step out through the door when Christian rises from his seat. "Promise me, Roni. Go back to Bellevue Springs and live your life the way you'd always intended. Don't go back to him."

I press my lips into a tight line knowing that no matter what, I'll never stop feeling this way about Nic, but Christian has a point. What kind of life is living on the run with a man who takes pleasure out of pain?

So instead of answering him, I wrap my arms around his large body and crush my face into his chest. "I love you, Christian," I tell him, pained at the forced way he curls his arms back around me. "Don't be a stranger." And with that, I pull out of his arms and walk right back out of his life, knowing that there's a good chance that I might never see him again.

CHAPTER 11
DOMINIC

Pain tears through me as I come to. I'm surrounded by bodies, but I focus on Sebastian's winced expression hovering over me as he jams a long pair of tweezers deep inside my chest.

My hand snaps up and I shove Sebastian away from me, yanking the tweezers out as I go. Pain rips through me, and I quickly notice the pool of blood on the bench beneath me. "Woah," Elijah says, grabbing my shoulders and forcing me back down, Kairo having to jump in and lend a hand. "What the fuck do you think you're doing? Stop fucking moving. There's a bullet lodged in your chest. Are you trying to get yourself killed? Again?"

"Fuck off," I grumble, attempting to push them off but after all the blood loss from the fucking bullet in my chest, I have no energy or strength to fight back. "Where's Roni? Tell me she's safe." The boys glance at each other and my worst fears are realized. "WHERE THE FUCK IS SHE?" I roar, fighting against their hold and getting absolutely nowhere.

Kairo moves in so that his face is all I see as he struggles to hold me down. "Christian took her, but he's not going to hurt her. He was trying to protect her."

"I was trying to protect her," I spit.

Sebastian scoffs, his sarcasm shining through bright and clear as he grumbles under his breath. "He didn't see it that way."

I glare at the fucker, trying really hard to remember that he's one of my best friends, one of my brothers. "You let her get away," I say, aiming my comments at all three of them while staring down Sebastian for his bullshit comments.

"Can you blame us?" Kairo says, pushing down harder than necessary just to be an ass as Sebastian leans into me, preparing to shove those godforsaken tweezers into my chest again. "You stood in front of Christian's fucking gun and played chicken. What did you expect was going to happen? She's his baby sister. She belongs with him, not here with us. If the tables were turned and that was Ocean, we all would have done the same thing, and you know it. You're lucky his aim was off and a bullet lodged in your chest was all you got."

I grunt in pain as the tweezers push into the hole in my chest. "I wouldn't fucking miss," I spit through a clenched jaw, trying desperately to ignore the pain tearing through me, but what other option do I have? It's not like my dumb ass can take a trip down to Breakers Flats Hospital and ask for help. "You. All. Let. Her. Go."

"She's not ours to hold onto," Kairo argues back. "You said yourself that she was bait for Christian. Well, good fucking job, you lured him in just as you wanted, but next time you want to play around with our fucking lives, a little warning would be nice."

Sebastian pushes a little harder and a roar of pain tears from my throat as I fight against the boys' hold. Three other Widows jump in and hold me down, keeping me pinned while Sebastian takes his fucking time, fishing around for the bullet that feels as though it's lodged against bone.

My body shakes as it begins to go into shock and the boys start working a little faster. "Bite down on this," Eli says, grabbing a discarded hoodie and bunching up the fabric before jamming it between my teeth.

I instantly bite down, desperately needing to focus on anything but the tweezers inside my chest. I can feel the metal dragging along the surface of the bullet and I groan, feeling as though I could throw up from the pain. It's not the first time I've had to sit in this very spot having my body searched for stray bullets, but fuck—maybe it's the six and a half years away from this life—it's never quite hurt so bad. This torture is worse than getting shot in the first place.

Sebastian clutches down on the bullet, and the boys all tense, knowing this is going to be the worst part. A bottle of pure alcohol sits on standby while someone's dirty shirt waits to be drenched in my blood.

This is going to be all sorts of fucked-up.

Sebastian meets my eyes, letting me know it's time and I nod, biting down on the hoodie harder, preparing for what's about to come. Not wanting to draw it out, he tugs hard and a throbbing pain soars through me. My chest burns and I scream out, the sounds muffled by the hoodie.

He has to give it three hard tugs before the bullet is finally dislodged from my chest. When I think I can finally relax, the alcohol is poured over me.

"FUCK," I grunt, spitting out the hoodie and balling my hands into tight fists, wishing I could slam them against one of these dickheads' faces to let them feel just an ounce of the pain I'm going through. Sure, they all look a little banged up from the battle we all just fought through, but none of them have a bullet wound or got stabbed.

Once the throbbing begins to ease, the boys pull back and give me space to breathe. I grab the bottle of who the fuck knows and lift it to my lips as Sebastian comes at me with a needle and thread. I take a hit from the bottle and as it goes down, I recognize the familiar sharp burn of vodka. Fuck, this ain't going to do shit. I need the heavy stuff. Vodka is a chick drink that exists only to make them act like fucking giggly bitches. This isn't going to help numb the pain, but nonetheless, I drink up, knowing that it's better than nothing.

I wait patiently as Sebastian stitches my chest and Eli takes a crack at the stab wound. I do everything in my power to think of anything but the needles piercing my skin over and over again and find that all I can think about is Roni. I have to get to her. I have to bring her back, but how? I'm not exactly in the right state to fight Christian again. I nearly didn't make it out of the last fight, let alone standing against him again.

The boys finish and I wait an extra twenty minutes before sitting up on the bench, waiting to replenish the blood I lost. My body aches in ways that no one should ever have to get used to, but I wear the pain as a badge of yet another battle that couldn't take me out.

Kairo comes at me with a bottle of water and painkillers. "Here, take these," he tells me, handing over the small pills that are bound to knock me the fuck out if I'm not careful. "They'll help take the edge off."

I take them greedily and throw them back. I've never understood those douchebags who refuse painkillers in their need to be high and fucking mighty. It sounds stupid to me. If there's something there to ease the pain and make life just that little bit easier, then I'm down. Why be in pain if you don't have to be? Using pain as self-punishment is a different story.

Once the pills make their way to the bottom of my stomach, I stand and look down at Kai. "Where's my car?"

"The fuck?" he grunts, flying to his feet beside me and catching my elbow. "What do you mean 'where's my car?' The fuck do you think you're going?"

"Where do you think?" I growl, glaring at the guy who I trusted to help keep Roni safe—and where she belongs. "I'm getting my girl and bringing her home."

"Dude," he says, slowly shaking his head with regret in his eyes.

"She's not your fucking girl. You took her from her home. She's with her brother now and I can guarantee that she's not coming back. I don't know what the fuck you think is going on between you two, but no chick I've ever met is willingly going to go back to the dickhead who kidnapped her and kept her locked in his secret little underground bunker."

I shake my head. "Exactly my fucking point, you don't know Roni, and you have no fucking idea what's going down between us. I wasn't fucking lying when I told you that I've been in love with her since I was sixteen years old. She's my fucking girl and she belongs wherever the fuck I am."

He narrows his eyes, watching me with curiosity. "What about Ocean? You spent two fucking years claiming that you were in love with her. You tried to talk her into marrying you, bro."

"Look, don't get me wrong here, I do love Ocean. I always have and I always will, but you know just as much as the boys do that what I had with Ocean wasn't real. She was always meant to be with that rich prick. With her, it was raw and fast like a burning candle that was always meant to sizzle out. With Roni, it's the fucking sun that only gets stronger with time. She's not sizzling out, bro. She hasn't for twelve years. She's the reason I threw myself so completely in with Ocean. I needed a distraction, someone to take my mind off her, and it worked for a while, but when I found her again in Bellevue Springs, I knew it was only a matter of time."

Kairo watches me for a moment, his brows raised as he stares, considering every last word. "You're serious about this?"

"So fucking serious that I'll walk into that fucking Wolf Den right now just to get her back."

Kai nods, and a second later, he's pulling a set of keys out of his pocket. "Then I'll drive. You're in no state to get behind the wheel. You'll fucking kill yourself and every fucker on the road before you can find her."

A grin stretches wide across my face and within seconds, I'm moving toward his car. I get into the passenger side and instantly put the chair right back to take some of the strain off my wounds. It's going to be a long fucking night. I'm already bleeding through the bandages the boys dressed my wounds with. I can't wait to see the extent of the infection I'll most likely get from this bullshit.

After letting the boys know what's going on, Kairo takes off down the road, and not actually being stupid enough to walk into the Wolf den, we head for Bellevue Springs. If she's not with Christian, then hopefully, she'll be home.

The drive to Bellevue Springs is longer than I could possibly bear, but for Roni, there's not a damn thing I wouldn't do. I really hadn't hoped to be back here so soon after the breakout, especially since my face is pretty well known around here and the fuckers with gold lining their pockets will call the cops the second they see me. The rules of Bellevue Springs are far different from the ones I grew up with.

I have to make this quick.

I pull on a black hoodie and cover my face as best as I can before slipping out of Kai's car and all but running to the entrance of Roni's apartment building, desperate for the shelter the building can offer.

Kai follows me in and I lead him up to Roni's apartment. We walk down the hall, and as we approach her place, our pace begins to slow.

Her door is open just a crack and it instantly sends chills sweeping through my chest.

A gun rests in my hand within seconds as Kai covers my back. We creep toward her apartment and I lean into the door. Reaching out, I silently push the door open with the tip of my gun.

I hear nothing from inside, and from where I stand at the door, I see nothing either, but that doesn't mean that no one is in there. It doesn't pay to be stupid.

Keeping my back to the wall, I creep into Roni's apartment and the first thing I notice is that the room is completely empty. No furniture, frames, not even those ridiculous little candles she had on the window sill when I came storming through here the first time.

It's a fucking shell.

My brows furrow but before I start thinking into it, Kai and I finish checking the apartment to make sure we're alone. I meet him back in the kitchen to find his face filled with the same questioning concern. "What the fuck is this?" he asks. "I thought she lived here. Where's all her stuff?"

I shake my head and walk over to the window, peering out to where her car used to be, but as the seconds tick by, it becomes startlingly clear.

She ran.

Christian let her go, probably told her some bullshit to scare her, and just like that, she's gone. I knew it was always an option, but fuck,

I didn't think she'd take it so willingly.

Why does it sting so fucking bad? Is that from the bullet or her betrayal? It's nearly impossible to tell; getting stabbed through the back would hurt less.

I step back into the center of her apartment, glancing around at the emptiness that seems to mimic the hollowness inside my chest. She's really gone.

I thought we were starting to build something again, learning to trust again, and finding that old fire that used to burn so brightly between us. I know it was only a week, but fuck, it's been one of the best weeks of my life.

She can't be gone. I have to get her back and I'll stop at nothing to find her, even if it means kidnapping her every fucking day for the rest of my life. I refuse to allow this shit to be over. How could I possibly live without that smile and that sarcastic as fuck fiery attitude that always seems to have something to say? Her body and her mind, but most of all, the passionate way that she loves to hate me, the way her nails sink into my skin, and the way her palm slaps across my face while we're fucking, reminding me that despite how things may seem, she's always been in charge.

Roni Russo is mine.

I glance back up at Kai and let out a breath. There's nothing I can do about it tonight, especially considering the gaping hole in my chest. "Let's get out of here," I tell him, "And do me a favor; stop by the liquor store and get every fucking bottle of bourbon they have. I'm going to need it."

CHAPTER 12

DOMINIC

The boys sit around me as I stare into the darkness of the warehouse. It's been two fucking days and they haven't left me alone for two seconds, apart from the few hours it took them to figure out who the fuck betrayed us to the Wolves. They dealt with it and were back in no time, probably terrified that I'll go and take my frustrations out on Christian and accidentally start another gang war. But what does it matter at this point? Maybe another gang war while I'm already down is exactly what I need to finally end this pathetic existence.

Look at me, sitting here in an empty warehouse, hiding out from the rest of the world, unable to show my face while my girl runs further and further from me.

I finish off yet another bottle of bourbon, knowing that at some point, I'm going to have to stop drinking and start getting on with my shit. I'm the leader of the Black Fucking Widows. I don't have time for moping in my creepy as fuck murder house. I should be out there planning a way to move against the Wolves without losing any more of my men.

Christian is going to pay for that shit.

When will it fucking end? It seems that no matter what either of us do, this war between us will always rage on. It's been going strong for over twenty years now. I doubt it'll be ending any time soon. I might as well get comfortable and prepare myself for a show. There should be movies made about this rivalry. It's one for the ages.

Launching the empty bottle across the warehouse, it slams against one of the many metal pillars, shattering into a thousand pieces. I have no doubt I'll have to clean that shit up tomorrow. The boys are more than happy to help me clean up after myself when it has something to do with the Widows, but when it's my own reckless bullshit, I'm out on my own.

The guys ignore me and keep on with their bullshit conversation, reminiscing about 'old times' that I wasn't even here for because my ass was locked up. Either way, I appreciate them if only to keep me from making a stupid fucking decision.

They fill me in on all the little ins and outs that I've missed about Ocean and her daughter, Storm, and just when I think I can't take another word, the alarm of the warehouse drops and screeches through the whole building.

The four of us pause, each of us glancing at the brother beside us and silently putting a game plan together. We're on our feet in seconds, mine slightly wobbly after the bottles of bourbon that I've downed over the past two days.

We instantly split up and get out of the center of the building, making the targets on our back not quite so obvious. We were sitting ducks chilling out in the middle of an abandoned warehouse like that. It was stupid, but I assumed no one could find me here.

Guess I was wrong, just like I was wrong about Roni.

My gun rests comfortably in my hand as I creep toward the front entrance of the building with Eli on the other side. Sebastian and Kairo head for the back roller door, making sure we have all exits covered, but I don't like it. The four of us should always stick together, though, in a building like this, it's near impossible.

I hear the familiar metal scratching of someone yanking at the lock on the front door and I glance over at Eli. Whoever this person is either has balls of steel or is really fucking stupid. I'll take option number two.

It's not the Wolves. They would have run at the first hint of the alarms being dropped, so that puts it down to drunken teenagers who are probably wanting to get in and trash the place. They're about to learn a really important lesson; don't fuck with Dominic Garcia.

Eli and I get closer and closer while listening to the sound of the chains recklessly being yanked away. We don't bother being careful. With the alarm screeching through the building, no one on the outside will be able to hear us.

We're covered in darkness, and as the chains finally come free, a grin pulls at my lips. This is exactly what I've been needing to get my mind off Roni.

The roller door begins to lift and I see a lone shadow standing at the other side with just the light from a cell phone. Without hesitation, I rush in.

My arm slips around the throat of the shadowed person as my gun presses up against the person's temple, and just as I go to squeeze my arm a little tighter, I get hit with the familiar scent of her fruity shampoo.

Roni freezes for a fraction of a second before racing up and tearing the gun out of my hand. "What do you think this is?" she demands, not daring to step out of my hold. "I come all the way back here and get hit with this bullshit?"

"Roni?" I question, hardly able to believe what I'm seeing as she slowly turns in my arm. The guys all stand around, checking that there's no other threat, and within seconds, discreetly walk over to their cars and fuck off out of here, leaving me gaping at the woman who has destroyed me while the alarm screeches through the warehouse.

She looks up at me with those big, pleading eyes. "I couldn't stay away," she whispers, her voice somehow heard over the alarm.

I don't wait a second longer before crushing my lips to hers and kissing her deeply. I scoop my hands under her body and lift her into my arms before walking back into the warehouse to where we'll be protected.

The alarm shuts off and I can't help but wonder if it was on some kind of timer or if Kairo has shut it off remotely. Either way, I don't really give a fuck, all that matters is the woman in my arms.

I pull the roller door down behind me and remind myself that I'm going to have to come back out here and lock it up properly but Roni is too important to pull myself away from right now.

I take her right through to the shitty bunker that we've been calling home and place her down on her feet, right before the bed, my lips still crushed in a furious battle with hers, each of us fighting for dominance.

My hands drop to her waist and I tear her shirt over her head, my fingers brushing over her soft skin. She's so fucking perfect, every inch, every strand of hair, every smart-ass comment that comes flying out of her mouth.

I fucking love it.

I throw her shirt aside, having absolutely no idea where it lands, and find her standing before me in a black lace bra and can't help but take a moment to appreciate the view. This bra won't exist in the next three seconds so I might as well enjoy it while I can. I don't know what it is about black lace on a woman, but fuck, it could bring me to my knees.

I reach around her and slowly strip her bra off, dragging the soft material down her arms to find her tits so plump and full, her nipples pebbled and begging for attention.

I'm not one to disappoint.

Roni silently watches every move I make as I brush my fingers over her skin and cup her perfect tits in my hand. I take her waist and lift her into my arms, and she instantly wraps her legs around me, bringing her tits right to my face.

I suck her nipple into my mouth and watch as her head tilts back in ecstasy. Her hands grip my shoulders before thinking better of it and peeling my shirt up between our bodies.

The movement has the material scraping against the bandages of my chest and waist and while the pain has me wanting to violently throw up, I focus all my attention on the one good thing in my life.

Bringing my lips back to hers, I take the two steps to the edge of the bed and lay her down before coming down on top of her. She sucks in a gasp and stops me halfway, staring at the bandages taking over a good portion of my chest and waist. "I hate that you got hurt like this," she says, tears filling her eyes as she takes it all in.

"I'm fine, baby. It's just a scratch."

She shakes her head as her eyes come back to mine, amusement shining brightly. "It's a bullet hole. You're an asshole for shrugging it off like that; it's definitely not just a scratch."

I grin and come down on top of her, bracing myself on my elbow to not crush her perfect little body. "Shut up and let me fuck you until you can't remember why the fuck you walked away to start with."

A brilliant smile stretches over her face and she lifts her head off the pillow, meeting her lips with mine. "What are you waiting for?"

Well, fuck me. Who am I to say no to an offer that?

My hands drop to the front of her pants and I drag the tight denim down her legs before stepping back off the end of the bed and watching her eyes flame with need as I pop the button of my jeans.

My pants fall to the ground and my cock springs free. I wrap my fingers around it, slowly working up and down as I watch my girl squirming on my bed. She clenches her thighs, desperately trying to relieve the ache pulsing between them, though I'm more than happy to help her out there.

As I lean down on the bed, her legs fall open and my tongue runs over my lips. Fuck, I want to taste her so bad but the thought of sinking my cock deep inside her sweet pussy and claiming her as my own is far too tempting.

Hell, we have all fucking night. I can do both, but first, I'm going to fuck her and show her exactly where she belongs.

Roni reaches up and hooks her arms around my neck, pulling me down to her, and as I go, I line myself up with her tight little pussy and sink deep inside of her.

Her soft, needy groan in my ear is enough to nearly bring me to the edge but I hold onto it, not daring to disappoint her with coming so soon. No, my girl deserves the fucking best and that's exactly what I'm going to give her.

"Fuck, Nic," she moans as I start moving, drawing back before pushing deeper and deeper, hitting all those spots that I know drive her wild. She tilts her head back on the mattress and I can't resist claiming her neck. My lips roam over her soft, sensitive skin and she clenches her eyes, her fingers digging in just the way she likes it. "Holy shit. Yes."

I reach down between us and as my cock slides in and out, torturing her with slow movements, I find her clit and apply just a bit of pressure before rubbing lazy circles.

I start picking up the pace with each thrust, hitting her just a little harder, a little faster. I watch as she bites down on her lip, her panting increasing as her moans continue slipping from between her lips.

Her pleasure is my fucking drug. Watching her face morph with need and undeniable desire is quickly becoming everything to me. I could fuck her all day for the rest of eternity and never get bored of it.

I've never fucked her slow like this, never watched as her body was pushed closer and closer to the edge. Don't get me wrong, I have fucked her in every way possible and watched as her orgasms have exploded around her, tearing her world apart, but this is a slow-burn, constantly building, getting stronger and stronger until she can't take the intensity any longer.

"Fuck, Roni. You're so fucking beautiful," I murmur, looking down at her gorgeous face as her eyes glisten with happiness, love, and desire.

She bites down on her lip and reaches up, running her thumb over my lips until I catch it in my mouth and bite down on the soft tip. "Whatever happened to 'shut up and let me fuck you?' "

"Changed my mind."

She shakes her head, grinning up at me with that cocky little attitude of hers. "Not going to happen," she tells me, curling her legs around my waist and forcing me deeper inside her. "You got my body all worked up and desperate, so fuck me like you mean it, or I'm going to do it myself."

I raise a brow, absolutely loving her fierce nature, but without missing a beat, I capture her hands from around my neck and lock them in one hand while hooking her leg up high over my hip. "Are you sure about this?" I ask, looking down at her wild, excited eyes. "If you want it rough, then that's what you'll get."

"Fuck me, Nic."

Well, damn.

Not wanting to disappoint my queen, I pull back and slam deep inside, stretching her as I go. She cries out, throwing her head back in pleasure and I feel her tightening around me. I go again, grunting and holding onto her.

I pick up my pace, slamming into her over and over again until she's screaming my name. Her fingers ball into tight fists and I know that she's dying to drag those nails down my back. I bring my hand down on her ass and she screams out again. "Oh God, YES!"

I give her exactly what she needs until finally, her tight little pussy is clenching down around me and she screams out my name. "Nic. FUCK."

I come hard, sending hot spurts of cum shooting inside her, but I don't stop moving, letting her ride out her orgasm on my cock until she finally goes limp beneath me.

I crash down on top of her, instantly regretting it as the pain soars through my chest, but it's so fucking worth it.

Roni crushes her lips to mine. "Shit, you've been holding out on me."

"Nah, babe," I say, smiling against her lips. "You just weren't ready for that."

"And now I am?"

"You tell me, baby," I say, rolling off to allow her to breathe properly. I pull her into my side and curl my arm around her sexy little body, my hand coming to a stop on her perfectly round ass. "I'm assuming that since you came back, you want this just as bad as I do. Are you ready for this? For you and me?"

She climbs up onto my chest, being careful not to venture anywhere near my bandages before she nods, meeting my eyes with the emotion pouring out of her in waves. "I didn't think I was," she tells me. "You were such an ass all week but I've realized that I fucking love that about you. You're so fierce and dominant and nothing has ever turned me on more."

Tears well in her eyes and I reach up to wipe them away. "What's wrong?" I murmur, hating how much those tears break me inside.

"I tried to run. I wanted to. Christian told me that this life with you wouldn't be much. I'll be constantly on the run and not able to have a proper life. He let me go and I started packing my things the second I got home, but I got twelve hours away before I realized how much of a mistake I was making. I'm in love with you, Nic, and I think on some level I always have been and I want to hate myself for feeling that way."

Those words are like magic to my ears and I can't help but cut her off, wanting nothing more than to pull her down and kiss her until we can't breathe. "Roni—"

"No ..." she says, stopping me so she gets a chance to finish the speech that she's obviously rehearsed on the long drive here. "I ... This isn't the life I ever envisioned for myself. I thought I was going to make it to the top and be this amazing version of myself who was lucky enough to start fresh. I left all this shit behind years ago and never looked back, but I was missing something."

"Me."

"No, dickhead. I was missing a fucking donkey," she laughs, playfully smacking my shoulder. "Of course, you."

I roll my eyes, my hand stinging to spank that perfect ass of hers again. "So, what are you going to do about it?"

"I'm going to hold on with both fucking hands and never let you go. Every day with you is an adventure and I'm not going to miss that for anything. Screw my brother and his need to tell me what I need to do with my life. I'm here now and I'm not going anywhere."

A grin stretches across my face and I grab hold of her, pulling her down to me, but before I get a chance to bring her lips to mine, she pulls back. "But listen, we need to get one thing straight." I raise a brow, knowing that whatever is about to come out of her mouth is going to be good. "I'm not some cheap whore who you can keep locked up in your little escape bunker. I'm a classy lady. I'm going to need a little more than this shithole. I mean, I'll be happy either way, I'm just saying …"

I laugh and pull her in, crushing her lips to mine in a bruising kiss as I finally feel at ease for the first time in years. "I'm working on it."

EPILOGUE

RONI

THREE YEARS LATER

I stare at my reflection in the small mirror of the sun visor as I sit, anxiously waiting in Nic's car. My knee bounces but I'm ready. I'm so fucking ready.

Nic glances over at me as he brings his car to a stop, his fingers curling around the steering wheel, turning his knuckles white. His lips lift into a cocky grin as his eyes rake over my body with a boyish excitement that has butterflies rising in my stomach. I love it when he looks at me like that. Even after three years of being officially together, I'm still the world to him, and I'll never get tired of that. "Screw this. Let me take you home and fuck you instead."

My gaze travels over his body, and damn it, I'd like nothing more than to bail and let him take me home, but if we don't do this now, we might not get another chance. "Stop looking at me like that," I tell him. "We're doing this."

A seriousness flashes through his eyes as he watches me. "It's gotta be fast," he reminds me for the millionth time as I run my hands down my body, double-checking that I strapped my gun to my thigh. It wouldn't be the first time that I ventured out and forgot it, leaving me in a shitty situation, but in my position, a gun is a must.

I roll my eyes. "I know." I've been playing this game with him for too long now not to know just how serious this is. If Nic is seen, his ass will be locked back up within seconds. We got close to losing him again last year but Nic is nothing if not a sneaky fucker. Since then, the cops have been instructed to shoot first, think later.

It's a war that has gone on and on for years, and so far, we've been ahead of the game. We've been able to buy our own house, which has stayed completely under the radar. We go out, we live our lives, and we run our fucking empire, but then there are times like this when they're hot on our trail ...

I see Kairo's car parked across the road while Sebastian's discreetly comes to a stop down the street. Nic glances out the window, meeting Kairo's stare, and nods, letting him know we're ready before turning his head and watching out my passenger side window, knowing that Sebastian and Eli would be watching us closely, waiting for our signal.

"There," Nic murmurs, pointing out our target that's half-hidden behind a fountain before glancing down at his watch. "Right. You ready?"

"Never been so ready."

Nic nods. "Let's do this."

With that, we bail out of Nic's car and run, sprinting toward the man as Kairo, Sebastian, and Eli do the same. Nic runs right by my side, and I sense his desperation to grab my hand to keep me from falling behind, but he wouldn't dare. He's protective as shit, but I'm a fucking boss ass bitch and I can carry myself. Besides, usually, I would keep up with him perfectly, but dressed like this, I'm at a loss.

The many familiar faces loitering in the street see us the second we break out of the car, and just like that, the hundred or so Widows who were available with zero warning start racing in behind us, always having our backs.

The man at the fountain sees us coming and, in an instant, starts preparing himself, glancing around at the many people heading his way.

We reach him in no time.

Nic pulls to a stop and I come in beside him as the crowd of Widows gathers behind us. "GO," Nic roars, rushing the man along to get this shit started as Sebastian, Kai, and Eli stand off to the side, exactly where they should be.

The man nods, looking mostly terrified but does exactly what he's been tasked to do. "We are gathered here today—"

"No. Vows, rings, kiss, done," Nic demands as something pulls on my dress.

I glance back to find Ocean standing behind me with her husband, Colton, who has their little girl, Storm, perched on his hip. She beams up at me as she straightens my wedding gown, making it absolutely perfect. "You look incredible."

I so desperately want to throw myself into her arms and thank her for coming to this shit show, but the celebrant is following Nic's demands as though his life depended on it. "Dominic, your vows," he prompts as Nic clutches my hands.

Nic stares into my eyes, and I realize that he has a speech made for this very moment. "I …" the sound of police sirens in the distance has his face dropping and panic soaring through me. "Fuck, um. I vow to love and cherish you as my queen until someone or something takes me out of this world."

I nod. "Same."

The priest looks between us, confusion marring his face. I'm sure he's never run a ceremony quite like this before. "Exchange of rings."

Kairo steps into Nic's side as the sirens get louder and hands him the rings that have been living peacefully inside his suit jacket pocket. Within the space of two seconds, Nic grabs my hand and slides the ring on before shoving his in my hand and prompting me to do the same. I don't even have a chance to look at it before the celebrant is continuing, clearly realizing that those sirens are meant for us. "Umm, I guess, I pronounce you husband and wife. Kiss your bride."

The sirens get obnoxiously louder, but this is one part of the ceremony that Nic and I will not be skimping on. He grabs me and pulls me in, curling his arms around my body before crushing his lips to mine and kissing me deeply.

The Widows cheer around us, drawing even more attention to us and as Nic pulls back from me, the celebrant holds out a piece of paper. "Sign here," he says, not allowing us the chance to just enjoy this moment, though, we're not exactly paying him to give us the full-on, lovey-dovey, hearts and roses kind of package. We weren't kidding about getting in and getting out. We can enjoy it later.

Nic grabs the pen out of his hand and signs his life away before handing it to me. The celebrant points to the section where I need to sign just as multiple cop cars come to a screeching stop, blocking off the street.

I slam the pen down on the papers as Nic hikes up my dress, yanking my gun out of its sheath. He slams it into my hand as all the Widows pull out their own.

Ocean yells out that she'll call me later and takes off with Colton, doing everything they can to keep their little girl safe before this turns into a shoot-out. The Widows create a barrier between us and the cops and as Nic takes my hand, he grins down at me. "Now it's time for the real show," he says, glancing up and indicating to the other side of the street where hundreds of Wolves begin pouring in, Christian standing front and center.

My big brother nods, giving me his approval and I can't help but smile. How is this day so fucked-up yet so damn perfect?

I adjust my gun in my hand and beam up at Nic, knowing he had everything to do with this. "Thank you," I whisper. "That means the world to me, but I hope it was all worth it. I hope we covered all the basics to make this wedding legal."

He shrugs his shoulders as the cops start yelling for us to put our weapons down, half of them turning around to face the Wolves, only just realizing that we're no longer the ones surrounded; they are.

"Beats me," Nic says. "We signed, kissed, and said our vows, and that's all that matters in my eyes."

I push up onto my tippy-toes and brush my lips over his before turning and looking out at the cops, knowing that my men will have our back. After all, I'm not just Nic's little plaything anymore. He did more than bring me over to the dark side. I stood up and found where I truly belonged in this world.

There's a reason Nic calls me his queen.

I'm the leader of the Widows now and these are my men, and while the cops have been non-stop searching for Nic, today they're here for me, and I've never been so excited.

Well, bring it on fuckers. I'm ready.

REJECTS PARADISE SERIES PLAYLIST

Game of Survival - Ruelle
I'm Gonna Show You Crazy - Bebe Rexha
Nightmare - Halsey
Never Tear Us Apart - Bishop Briggs
Bird Set Free - Sia
Helium - Sia
Dusk Till Dawn - Zayn feat Sia
Heaven - Julia Michaels
Graveyard - Halsey
Bad Bitch - Bebe Rexha
Love Drug - G-Easy feat Halsey
Hurricane - Tommee Profitt
Unloveable - Delacey
Power - Isak Danielson
Cruel Intentions - Delacey feat G-Easy
Not Afraid Anymore - Halsey
Unstoppable - Sia
Monsters - Tommee Profitt
Can't Help Falling In Love - Tommee Profitt
Angel Cry - G-Easy feat Devon Baldwin
Bad At Love - Halsey
Creep - G-Easy feat Ashley Benson
In The End - Tommee Profitt
Wicked Game - Daisy Gray
Haunted - Beyonce
Gasoline - Halsey
I Feel Like I'm Drowning - Two Feet
Twisted - Two Feet
Wild Horses - Bishop Briggs
The Fire - Bishop Briggs
Killer - Vallerie Broussard

121

122

Thanks for reading!

If you enjoyed reading this book as much as I enjoyed writing it, please consider leavinge a review.

For more information on Rejects Paradise, find me on Facebook or Instagram –

www.facebook.com/SheridanAnneAuthor

www.instagram.com/Sheridan.Anne.Author

OTHER SERIES BY SHERIDAN ANNE

www.amazon.com/Sheridan-Anne/e/B079TLXN6K

YOUNG ADULT / NEW ADULT - ROMANCE

The Broken Hill High Series (5 Book Series + Novella)

Haven Falls (7 Book Series + Novella)

Broken Hill Boys (5 Book Novella Series)

Aston Creek High (4 Book Series)

Rejects Paradise (4 Book Series)

Black Widow (A Rejects Paradise Novella)

Boys of Winter (4 Book Series)

NEW ADULT ROMANCE

Kings of Denver (4 Book Series)

Denver Royalty (3 Book Series)

Rebels Advocate (4 Book Series)

CONTEMPORARY ROMANCE

Play With Fire (Co-Author - Dusty Lambert)

Until Autumn (Happily Ever Alpha World)

URBAN FANTASY - PEN NAME: CASSIDY SUMMERS

Slayer Academy (3 Book Series)